BETRAYAL OF TRUST

DeAnna Julie Dodson

AnniesFiction.com

Books in the Sweet Intrigue series

Library of Congress-in-Publication Data
Betrayal of Trust / by DeAnna Julie Dodson
p. cm.
I. Title
                    2020944665

AnniesFiction.com
(800) 282-6643
Annie's Sweet Intrigue™
Series Creator: Shari Lohner
Series Editor: Lorie Jones

10 11 12 13 14 | Printed in China | 9 8 7 6 5 4 3 2 1

Julianne Montgomery had always heard that you could never go home again. She understood that better now than she ever had before. Why in the world had she believed that moving back to Springfield, Illinois, would help anything?

Dealing with the death of her husband, David, was the most difficult thing she'd ever faced. It certainly wasn't something she could expect to do in five months.

When she'd returned to her hometown, Julianne had even been foolish enough to imagine buying her parents' old house, but it wasn't on the market. Besides, the house would have been way out of her price range, and it would have required too much maintenance.

The house she'd finally settled on, mostly because it was a steal of a deal, was too large for one person. If her husband were here, they might have needed the extra space one day for the children they'd dreamed about having. Of course, if David were alive, she wouldn't have moved to begin with. They'd still be living in their house in Chicago, he'd be working for the IRS, Julianne would be trying to make it as an artist, and her life would have some meaning.

Julianne drove her gray Honda Accord into the nearly vacant two-car garage, glad she didn't have to brave the rain to get into the house. When she was growing up in Springfield, June had often been one of the rainiest months. It had rained on her wedding day seven years ago. Julianne and David had dashed hand in hand to the car, only to find that his best man had locked all the doors. She remembered standing there with her new husband, both of them laughing as the downpour soaked them to the skin and their friends pelted them with sodden rice.

Now the rain was gray and sad, and she never went out in it.

Sighing, she shut off the car engine and pushed the button to close the garage door. Then she gathered her purse and the takeout Chinese food she'd picked up and entered the house.

After her old house had burned down, she'd used all the money from the insurance settlement to buy and furnish this one. A month later, it still didn't feel like home. Instead, it seemed more like a hotel suite or a furniture showroom. Not that it was particularly fancy, but she hadn't put much thought into decorating it. She hadn't put herself into it. She'd simply bought a modern furniture grouping in black lacquer from the store, artwork and all. Her own paintings had been lost in the fire along with everything else.

Julianne sat down in the living room in front of the television, turned on an old movie that she had already seen numerous times, and ate her dinner. The rain and the low chatter in the film lulled her, and she dozed off shortly after finishing the food.

The wail of electric guitars jolted her awake, and it took her a moment to realize it was her sister's ringtone. Julianne muted the television, jumped off the sofa, and scrambled in her purse for her phone. She answered right before it went to voice mail.

"I was about to hang up and call back," Dannie said.

"Sorry. I fell asleep on the couch." Julianne pushed a thick strand of blonde hair behind her ear and sat down again. "What's up?"

"Are you depressed?" Dannie asked. "A lot of people who are depressed sleep a lot. Have you been sleeping a lot?"

"No, but it's been a busy day, and I dropped off watching a movie," Julianne said. "It's not a big deal."

"You've been through so much in the past few months," Dannie continued. "I wouldn't be surprised if you were depressed. I think you should talk to someone."

"Are you referring to a psychiatrist?"

"It's nothing to be ashamed of," Dannie assured her. "I've been in therapy since Mom died. It was hard to lose her. I miss her so much."

Their mother had passed away two months ago. Julianne and David had taken care of Mom for nearly four years while she'd been ill. Dannie had her own life in Seattle. She had rarely visited, and she hadn't even talked to Mom on the phone very often. To Julianne, it sounded strange that Dannie was missing her so much now.

Julianne bit back the words she wanted to say. Instead, she replied, "I miss her too, but I'm okay. I'm trying to learn my new job and get used to my new house, and none of it feels right."

"Some people don't even realize they're depressed," Dannie persisted.

"I'm trying to get through it," Julianne said. "I miss David and Mom, and I wish I still had the house I loved and my own things."

"I can't imagine how hard it's been for you," Dannie said. "Losing David and Mom and then your house. Evan always tells me that—"

"Who's Evan?" Julianne asked, interrupting her sister. She wondered what had happened to Antonio. Or was it Cal?

"Oh, I haven't told you about him, have I?" Dannie asked. "He's the greatest guy. I met him at a sandwich shop. He's a poet. I mean, he was there making sandwiches, but that's temporary. He's the most profound person I've ever met, and he's only twenty-two."

Julianne stifled a sigh. Dannie was thirty-eight, six years older than she was.

"I was feeling sad about Mom," Dannie said, "and he told me—"

The doorbell rang.

Julianne stood and headed toward the front door. "I'm sorry, but there's somebody here. I've got to go."

"But I didn't get to tell you what Evan said about Mom and this bird he saw," Dannie protested.

"You can tell me what he said later."

The doorbell rang again.

"I have to go. Talk to you soon." Julianne disconnected and looked out the peephole to see who was at the door. She frowned. It was Larry Spielmann, her next-door neighbor. Still, he'd rescued her from the conversation with her sister. She opened the door.

"I, uh, saw you drive in, and I thought—well, Mother thought you might like to come over and have dinner with us." Larry grinned, and his dark eyes were pitifully hopeful behind his thick glasses. "She made a meat loaf, peas and carrots, and fruit salad. We have ice cream if you don't like fruit salad, but Mother didn't think that would be good since it's rainy tonight, and it might make you feel cold."

"That's so thoughtful of you both," she said, giving him a warm smile. "But I already ate. It was Chinese takeout, nothing nearly as good as your mother's cooking."

He swallowed, making his prominent Adam's apple bob. "I told Mother she should have called you ahead of time, but she said it wouldn't hurt anything to ask in case you didn't have anything to eat in the house."

"That's sweet of her," Julianne said. "And it's nice of you to come all the way over in the rain to ask me. I hope you didn't get too wet."

Larry's dark hair was plastered to his head, and his cotton shirt was clinging to his thin frame. "Oh, not at all." He crossed his arms over his chest. "It's just next door, and it's not that cold out here."

"No, but you should probably change into dry clothes as soon as possible," she advised.

He ducked his head. "I'm sure Mother will be after me about that as soon as I get home."

"Well, it was good of you to stop by." Julianne started to slowly close the door. "Please thank your mom and tell her how much I appreciate her kindness."

"I will," Larry said. "Next time I'll make sure she checks with you to see if you've already eaten."

"Thanks again," she said. "Have a good evening."

"Bye," he said, a touch of wistfulness in his tone.

Julianne closed the door and peered into the peephole again. She watched Larry trudge down the walkway until she couldn't see him any longer.

She locked the door and the dead bolt. Larry was a nice guy. Sure, he was thirty-seven and lived with his mother. Rhoda Spielmann was nice too. She was always checking on Julianne and bringing her something to eat. The way Julianne had fallen into this house and her job, one she didn't feel the least bit qualified for, it somehow wouldn't have surprised her to have fallen into the perfect romance too. But Larry wasn't her type, and she couldn't imagine falling for anyone after being married to David for seven years.

Julianne walked over to the picture that hung above the fireplace. It was their wedding portrait. Of course, the photograph in their own house had burned up along with everything else in the fire, but this one had belonged to her mom. It was the only personal picture in the room. It was the only one that mattered.

She hardly recognized herself with her hair in golden ringlets that cascaded down the back of her head. David stood behind her, his arms around her as they both held the bridal bouquet. He was so handsome in his tuxedo. They were flattering to most men anyway, but he'd been built to wear one with his tall and lean frame.

On their wedding day, he'd still been as fit as when he'd enlisted in the Marines.

Moving closer to the picture, she reached one hand toward it. Julianne wished she could touch his face, stroke the loosely curled brown hair with a light touch of the sun in it, and trace the curve of his lip with her finger. There was laughter in his gray eyes, even though he wasn't smiling. The photographer had cracked jokes constantly, but she couldn't remember exactly what he'd said when he snapped this photo.

"Stop looking back," she warned herself. "There are things to do."

Was that true? Julianne blew out a deep breath and scanned the room. The house was spotless. She'd eaten her dinner and thrown away the containers. Her movie was still going with the sound muted, but she already knew what they were saying. The thought of watching it again was suddenly not as comforting as it had been. Maybe Dannie was right. Julianne might be depressed. Or perhaps she was simply empty.

It felt lonely rattling around the large house, and Julianne wondered once more if she should adopt a pet to keep her company. Her mother had suggested it after David passed away, but Julianne had dismissed the idea. A year ago, she and David had lost their sweet cat, Andy, and they'd never had the heart to get another one.

She thought about Mom's other piece of advice. Whenever Julianne had moped around, her mom had always said, "If you're feeling down, do something to help someone else." She could definitely do that for Rhoda and Larry.

The other day, Julianne had gone to a bookstore. While she was browsing, she'd come across some secondhand books and magazines that she thought her neighbors might like, so she bought them. The box of reading materials was still in her car. She'd forgotten about it when Larry stopped by.

She went out to the garage and opened the trunk. It was empty except for two boxes. She took out the box of books and magazines and set it on the mostly empty shelf against the garage wall.

The other box was battered, and it contained a few emergency supplies in case she had car trouble. She smiled wistfully at the box itself. Jeff Macklin, one of David's coworkers at the IRS, had given it to her at the funeral. It had contained David's belongings from the office.

There hadn't been much inside the box. There was a cheaply made rug that was far too garish to use in the house. She couldn't imagine why David had kept it in his office, but she couldn't bear to get rid of it, so she left it inside the box in the trunk.

Besides the rug, the box had held a notebook full of notes and figures, a small framed photo of her sitting under a tree, and David's black coffee mug with a large white ampersand on it. To them, that ampersand meant David and Julianne, together always.

Now the mug sat on a shelf in one of the kitchen cabinets. The picture had been removed from its frame and was stuck on the refrigerator with a magnet. The notebook was stored in the bedroom she'd made into an office. And the rug was stuffed inside the box it had come in and left in the trunk.

"Stop looking back," she told herself again as she slammed the trunk shut.

Julianne carried the box of books and magazines into the house. Even though she didn't think she needed an umbrella, she grabbed one anyway to keep from giving Rhoda something to worry about.

By the time Julianne arrived at the porch of the house next door, she was glad she'd brought the umbrella with her. The rain fell in diagonal gray sheets, and she was soaked to the knees. She shook out the umbrella and leaned it against the wall next to the black door, then rang the doorbell.

Their cocker spaniel, Buttons, started barking.

Larry opened the door and gaped at Julianne for a moment. "Oh, hi," he said finally.

Buttons whined and beat her tail on the tile entryway, quivering with the pure excitement of having a visitor.

"Hush, Buttons," Larry told the dog, then gave Julianne a shy smile. "We went ahead and started eating. We didn't think you were coming."

Julianne shifted the increasingly heavy box in her arms. "I'm sorry for interrupting. I should have known you'd be having dinner, but right after you left, I remembered I had this box for you and your mother."

"Mother, it's Julianne from next door," Larry called over his shoulder. "She has something for us."

"Well, ask her in," Rhoda replied. "Don't make her stand outside in the rain."

"That's okay," Julianne said. "I only wanted to drop it off."

"Is it heavy?" Larry asked as he reached for the box.

"Yeah," Julianne admitted, then relinquished it. "Anyway, tell your mom I thought she'd like the books and magazines. If there are some she's not interested in, she can give them away to someone else or donate them."

"I'm sure she'd like to—"

"Larry, tell her to come in," his mother called again. "I'd like to thank her."

Larry shrugged sheepishly and stepped aside so Julianne could enter the house.

Buttons immediately jumped on her.

Julianne leaned down to rub her ears. "Hello, sweetie. Come on. Let's go inside."

The dog's whole body wriggled in delight.

Larry led Julianne through the small living room. She was reminded of her grandmother's house that had been packed with mismatched furniture and various mementos accumulated over a lifetime. She scanned a collection of porcelain thimbles from different states and a few bowling trophies prominently displayed on the mantel. One entire wall featured framed family portraits. Many of the pictures showed Larry as a small boy with big eyes, and some were of a paunchy, balding man with a gap-toothed smile. Julianne assumed he was the late Mr. Spielmann.

In the kitchen, Rhoda was sitting at the oak table in her wheelchair, a plateful of meat loaf and peas and carrots in front of her.

Rhoda smiled. "I'm so glad you changed your mind. Please sit down. Larry, bring our guest a plate."

Buttons plopped down at the woman's feet.

"Thank you," Julianne said. "It smells wonderful, but like I told Larry, I already ate. I stopped by because after he left, I remembered that I had picked up some things for you and Larry at the bookstore. I know you enjoy reading and knitting."

Larry set the box on the table beside his mother.

Rhoda opened it. "Oh, look at all these novels and knitting magazines." She held some out to her son. "Here are some of those computer magazines you like."

"I don't keep up with the latest developments, so they're probably outdated," Julianne said. "But my husband enjoyed reading those magazines."

"I'll check them out," Larry said, taking them from his mother. "Sometimes what they predict with new technology and how it actually turns out can be pretty entertaining."

"Anyway, I saw them there," Julianne said. "I didn't know what you'd like to read."

"No, these are great," Larry said. "You didn't have to bother."

"It was no bother," Julianne insisted.

"It was so thoughtful of you," Rhoda said. "What do I owe you?"

"Nothing at all," Julianne said, feeling her dark mood lift at the delight on the older woman's face. "I wanted to get them for you. You and Larry have been so nice to me since I moved here, and I wanted to do a little something to tell you how much I appreciate it."

Rhoda took Julianne's hand and squeezed it, her brown eyes shining. "It wasn't anything. Just what neighbors and friends do. And with the troubles you've had, we couldn't let you sit in that big house by yourself all the time. It's not natural."

"Well, I'd better go," Julianne said. "Enjoy your dinner."

"You can at least sit down and have dessert with us," Rhoda said.

"No thanks," Julianne said. "I have some things to do, and I need to get to work early in the morning."

"You seem tired," Rhoda said, a mixture of pity and concern in her eyes. "I wish you'd accept my offer to use our cabin. I'd feel much better if you got away for a few days. You already have the key."

"I appreciate it," Julianne said, remembering the rusted key in her purse.

"We haven't been there much since my poor Marvin died," Rhoda continued, "but it's stocked and cozy. Sangchris Lake is so pretty, and it's not even an hour away."

"It's not right on the lake," Larry put in. "But the area is nice and quiet, and nobody will bother you there."

"It sounds great," Julianne said. "But I don't have any vacation time at my new job yet. Maybe I'll take you up on it later."

Rhoda smiled. "You're welcome to use it anytime. Let me know if you decide to go, and make sure you lock it when you're done. I don't think anyone would get inside, but I don't want to take any chances."

"Thank you." Julianne squinted out the kitchen window. The rain was coming down harder. "I should get going before I have to swim home."

"You'd better walk with her, so she gets in all right," Rhoda told her son.

"I'll be fine," Julianne insisted. "I don't want Larry to get wet too."

"Get her some fruit salad to take home," Rhoda added as if Julianne hadn't spoken.

Larry dutifully went to the avocado-green refrigerator and removed a container.

"No, honestly," Julianne said. "I wouldn't want you to go to any trouble."

"It's no trouble," Rhoda assured her. "Not at all. Bring back the bowl when you're through. Put some plastic wrap on it, Larry, just to be sure."

Larry transferred a healthy serving of fruit salad from the container to a bowl and covered it with plastic wrap.

A few minutes later, fruit salad in hand and Larry in tow, Julianne arrived at her own front porch. She wished she'd remembered to leave the porch light on, but there was enough of a glow from her curtained front windows for her to see to unlock the door.

"Thanks," she said to Larry, taking charge of the umbrella he'd held over their heads on the trip. "On second thought, maybe you should take this. I can pick it up when I return your mom's bowl."

"It's all right. I'll run fast. Thanks for the magazines and stuff." With a wave, Larry bounded into the rain. He waved at Julianne again before ducking into his house.

Leaving the umbrella on the porch to dry, Julianne entered the house and locked the door. She headed straight for the kitchen, grabbed a spoon from the silverware drawer, and returned to the couch. The movie was still playing.

As Julianne ate the fruit salad and gazed at the TV screen, she decided that her mom had been right about helping others. She was grateful for the kindness of her neighbors and happy to have done something for them, even something as minuscule as giving them a box of secondhand books and magazines.

When she finished the fruit salad, she set the bowl aside and ended up falling asleep on the couch again before the end of the movie.

Julianne didn't know what woke her. Maybe it was the thunder and lightning. From the stiffness in her neck, she guessed she'd been asleep for two or three hours. Maybe more. Everything was dark. She hadn't turned out the lights before she dozed off, so the power must have gone out.

"Great," she muttered, staggering to her feet.

Julianne shuffled toward the bedroom to retrieve the flashlight in her nightstand. Somehow she made it to the nightstand without running into anything or stubbing her toes. As she opened the drawer and picked up the flashlight, another boom shook the house. In the blinding flash of lightning, against the cream-colored curtains that covered the French doors across the back wall, she saw the silhouette of a man.

Her heart pounded, and she couldn't move. Holding her breath, she aimed the flashlight toward the doors.

The intruder wore a soaked T-shirt, and the loose curls of his hair were plastered to his head. He took a step toward her, one hand outstretched, the other clutching a gun. "Don't scream," he whispered hoarsely.

Then the gun thudded to the carpet, and the man fell headlong across the bed.

Julianne gaped at him, hardly able to breathe.

It was David.

The lights flickered back on, and Julianne could see David clearly now. He was pale and shivering, soaked with rain and blood.

It didn't make any sense. David was dead. She'd seen the police report and the burned-out wreckage of the car. She'd sat stone-faced through his funeral and then felt numb as everyone told her how sorry they were. They assured her that she didn't want to see the body, and she had agreed. She had wanted to remember him as he was, warm and laughing and alive.

Alive.

David was still alive.

Her hand trembled as she reached out to touch his face. His skin was cold to the touch, but his breath was warm. He truly was alive.

"David," Julianne whispered, noticing the pool of deep red that was seeping out underneath him. She had no idea how her dead husband could possibly be here. But it didn't matter. Right now, David needed her help. She couldn't let him bleed to death.

Julianne ran into the bathroom, snatched four big towels, and brought them back to the bed.

David didn't move when she rolled him over, not even when she pulled up his once-white T-shirt and stuffed a towel under his left side, where all the blood was coming from.

He had been shot. She had to call an ambulance and the police. No, she had to keep him alive first. She had to stop the bleeding.

Julianne put another towel on top of the wound and pressed

down with both hands, watching as crimson spread across the delicate ivory.

He opened his eyes wide, evidently unable to hold back a cry of pain.

"I'm sorry," she said desperately. "I'm going to call an ambulance for you right now."

"Don't," David gasped, clutching her bloody hand with his. "Please don't call anybody."

"You need medical help, or you'll die," Julianne insisted. "I don't know how to get a bullet out or how to keep you from bleeding to death."

"You're doing fine," he assured her, trembling and holding her hand tighter. "The bullet only nicked my side, so it doesn't need to be removed. Help me stop the bleeding. Keep pressure on it for five minutes. That should be long enough. Don't worry. It'll be okay."

"Tell me what happened," she sobbed, pressing harder on the towel. "Where have you been all this time? If somebody shot you, I should tell the police."

"No," David said, his expression fierce and determined. "You can't say a word to anybody. No one can know I'm alive. Please do what I ask. Trust me."

Julianne stared at him. David had been gone for five months, letting her believe he was dead. He'd ripped her life into a million pieces, and now he wanted her to trust him?

"You could die if I don't get somebody," Julianne said, trying to keep her whirring thoughts on the task at hand. "What if you go into shock? You're cold, and you've lost a lot of blood."

"Just help me now," he pleaded. "I promise I'll explain everything later."

"You can't promise you won't die."

"The bleeding is already stopping," David said.

Startled, Julianne glanced down. The towel was soaked, but when she pulled it back, she saw the bleeding had slowed to a trickle. "Let me at least take you to a clinic."

"They'd have to report it, and that could be worse for me than bleeding to death." He grimaced. "Worse for you too."

"For me? Why? Tell me what's going on."

David squeezed her hand. "Let me rest for a few minutes. I'll tell you everything. Soon." His long lashes fluttered to his pale cheeks. "Please . . ." His hand went limp in hers.

"Don't die," she whispered, pushing his still-dripping hair away from his face. "Please don't die."

Julianne peeked under the towel again. The bleeding had stopped. As carefully as she could, she situated him the right way on the bed and slid a pillow under his head. She put a fresh towel under him and tossed the two soaked ones into the bathtub. Then she washed the blood from her hands and arms and rinsed them in alcohol.

She had to do something to keep the wound from getting infected. The alcohol would have to do that too. She was afraid David might go into shock from the pain if she used it on him, but she didn't know what else to do.

After retrieving more towels, a bowl of hot water, and alcohol, Julianne returned to the bedroom. She set everything down on the nightstand and leaned down to him, softly calling his name.

David didn't respond, but he was breathing.

She pressed her hand to his cheek. At least it didn't feel as clammy as it had. She dipped the folded corner of one towel into the hot water and swiped it across his side. He didn't stir, so she moved closer to the wound.

David still didn't open his eyes or move.

When the wound was cleaned up, it didn't look so bad. Maybe it wasn't much more than a nick, like he said. The bullet had definitely gone in through the front, but it had come out on the side, judging by the exit hole. At that angle, maybe it hadn't actually hit much more than skin.

Julianne moved a bit closer so she could see better. He was bleeding slightly again, and she wondered if she should apply the alcohol. She had to do something to prevent the wound from getting infected before she tried to bandage it.

After pouring alcohol on a towel, she gingerly touched it to the wound. David didn't flinch, and she poured on a little more and pressed it along his side. From what she could tell, he wasn't feeling anything, so she poured alcohol directly into the wound. He moaned softly, and she added more, letting it soak the towel under him. He groaned and tried to pull away. She held him still, glad he wasn't actually conscious.

"Shh," Julianne soothed as she started bandaging him.

He didn't move.

She padded the entrance and exit wounds with two folded-up washcloths and then bound them into place with a few strips torn from a flat sheet. It was primitive, but it would have to do.

Julianne knew it was a terrible idea to let David stay here without the help of a medical professional, but what if he was telling the truth? What if they were both in some kind of danger? And what kind of danger? The same danger that had caused him to fake his own death?

She managed to remove his T-shirt without having to cut it off. It was soaked with rain and blood, but there wasn't a bullet hole in it. He must have put it on after he was shot, but when was that? Where was that? She had so many questions that she didn't know where to start.

Sitting down on the bed next to David, Julianne studied his ashen face, the line between his eyebrows, and his hand that clutched the pillow beside his head. The knuckles were bruised and scraped.

There were bruises and scrapes on his chest, stomach, and arms that appeared as fresh as the ones on his hand. On both of his hands. She couldn't help wondering if the man he'd fought with had been the one who shot him. What had happened to that man? Was he after David now?

A droplet of rainwater ran from David's hair and down the side of his neck, and she reached over to wipe it away. Then the touch became a caress. He was alive. She still couldn't quite believe it. It didn't feel real. Maybe she'd wake up in a minute and be here alone with nothing but the beating of the rain on the roof for company.

But no, David was really here. He was cold and wet, and he needed to be taken care of.

Julianne removed his sodden tennis shoes and jeans and dried him off as best she could with one of the unused towels. David's body shook. Trying to move him as little as possible, she worked the comforter out from underneath him and covered him with a couple of quilts from the chest at the foot of the bed. As gently as she could, she lifted his head and replaced the soaked pillow with the one from the other side of the bed.

After he was out of his wet clothes, he seemed to rest easier. The line between his brows smoothed out, and he stopped shaking.

"Where have you been?" Julianne murmured, pushing a dark strand of hair off his forehead. Tears spilled down her cheeks. "What have you been doing all this time? Why did you leave? I've missed you so much. Please be all right."

His answer was a long, deep breath as he settled more deeply into the bed.

She slid her hand down his stubbled cheek to his neck, finding his pulse. It was slow and steady. He was alive.

Pushing down her roiling emotions, Julianne focused on what to do next. She picked up the gun and stowed it on the top shelf of her bedroom closet. Then she gathered his filthy clothes and shoes, along with the towels, comforter, and pillowcase, and stuffed them into the washing machine. The detergent claimed to be able to remove even the toughest stains, and she hoped it would deliver on its promise. Meanwhile, she would see if the spot remover she'd bought for the carpet was any match for bloodstains.

By the time she removed the stains from the carpet, the laundry was ready to go into the dryer. To her amazement, everything came out clean. The comforter, the towels, and the pillowcase weren't ruined. David's clothes appeared worn, but they would be good enough for him to wear until they could get him something else.

Julianne loaded the dryer and pushed the button to start it, then stood there with her hands braced against it as it whirled and shook, biting her lip to keep from crying again. David was alive. He was here.

She closed her eyes and swallowed hard. He was here, but what did that mean? Was he here to stay? Or was she soon to be alone—deeply, achingly alone—again?

Julianne went to the living room and collapsed onto the couch. She sat there for a long time, lost in her thoughts.

When the dryer buzzed, she took out the comforter. It was warm and soothing. Maybe David would feel better to have it over him now. Even though it was June, his skin had felt so cold when he'd first come in out of the rain.

She folded his clean clothes and stacked them on a nearby chair. Then she carried the comforter to the bed and spread it over him. It didn't appear as if he'd moved since she'd left him there. His hair had dried into its usual curls, but they were still very dark, nearly black. Why had he been dyeing it? She couldn't help touching him. She couldn't help making sure he was real.

She whispered his name, and he finally stirred.

David didn't open his eyes, but he was trying to say something.

"What is it?" Julianne asked. She couldn't make out any words, but whatever it was, it was obviously urgent. "What's going on?"

He shook his head.

"It's all right." She took his hand between both of her own. "Go to sleep now. You're safe."

David remained quiet.

Julianne sat down at the head of the bed, still with his hand in hers, and closed her eyes, telling herself it was only for a second.

The next thing she knew, it was light outside and David was burning up. "Oh, please, Lord, what do I do?" She eased his hand out of hers and stood.

He opened his eyes.

Julianne panicked when she noticed his gray eyes were glassy. Running to the bathroom, she found the thermometer. She rushed to the bed and took his temperature. It wasn't good. If she couldn't get him cooled down quickly, she would have to call an ambulance no matter what he wanted.

She grabbed a couple of the towels she had taken out of the dryer and soaked them in cold water. After wringing them out, she used them to wipe down David's chest and arms and face, praying all the while.

After a few minutes, she tried the thermometer again. He was a little cooler now.

"Thank You," Julianne breathed. She sat on the bed with his head in her lap.

He exhaled heavily and nestled against her.

Gazing at him, she tenderly stroked his hair. For a long time, she didn't move, afraid that he would disappear at any moment.

When her alarm went off, David jerked awake and struggled to sit up.

Julianne held him there as she shut the alarm off. "It's all right. You don't have to get up. It's Saturday."

Actually, it was Tuesday and she had to get up.

He stared at her as if he'd never seen her before.

"I can't go to work." She reached around David and grabbed her phone. "Jim will be annoyed with me for missing today."

Jim Webber was her boss at Carroll, James, and Webber, and Julianne was supposed to help him prepare for an important meeting today.

Julianne hated to disappoint Jim. He had made her feel welcome at the investment company from the moment he'd hired her as his administrative assistant, despite her lack of qualifications. She'd been working for him for about a month, and so far, he didn't seem to mind paying her a generous salary while she learned her administrative duties. Julianne was very thankful to have landed such a great job.

It was too early for Jim to be in the office, and she was glad she got his voice mail so he wouldn't be able to ask her any questions. Even so, her voice quavered when she left a message. "Jim, this is Julianne. I know I was supposed to help you prepare for the meeting today, but I can't come in. I'm feeling awful, and I think I have food poisoning. I'm sorry. I'm at home, so call me if you need anything."

Julianne hung up and returned her phone to the nightstand. She knew she couldn't leave David alone in his condition, but she couldn't help but feel guilty about taking a sick day from work.

When she touched his cheek, David felt warm but not quite as warm as before.

He opened his eyes at the touch, but this time he seemed to know her. "Sorry," he croaked. "I didn't think it was so bad."

"Do you want some water?" Julianne asked.

"Yeah, please." David gave her an apologetic grin. "I guess you weren't exactly expecting me."

"No, I wasn't." Suddenly Julianne couldn't think of anything but that he'd disappeared, evidently of his own volition, and allowed her to believe he was dead for five whole months. She left the room and filled a glass of water. When she returned, she held the glass as he drank.

"That's good," David gasped as a few drops of water spilled down his chin.

Julianne set the nearly empty glass on the nightstand. "How do you feel?"

"I've felt better," he answered. "And worse. Just last night, in fact. I want to tell you—"

"Let me check your side," she interrupted, not wanting him to explain.

David rolled over with a grunt. "It's not too bad, is it?"

"The bullet went through like you told me," Julianne said, "but I think you should see a doctor."

"No," he said, pulling away.

"All right, no doctor," she relented. "Now let me get a closer look."

David didn't say anything, but he let her examine him.

Julianne tried to remove the makeshift bandage, but dried blood had glued it to the wound. She had to soak the bandage in alcohol to get it off, and she could tell from David's expression that it was extremely painful. "I'm sorry, but I don't know what else to do."

"It's fine," he insisted. "I'm sure it'll be all right."

She peeled the bandage away from the wound. His side was red and puffy and very bruised, but there wasn't any more blood.

"You've always been a good nurse," David told her as she bandaged him again.

"You never were much of a patient," Julianne answered.

With another grin, he went back to sleep.

By the time David woke up, she had showered and changed into a pair of jeans and a pink T-shirt.

"I like you in pink," he said, stretching.

"You seem better," Julianne said, ignoring the compliment. He still appeared feverish, so she picked up the thermometer.

"No, I want to—"

"Don't talk," she said. "Instead of arguing with me, you should be figuring out how you're going to explain why you're here and exactly what you've been doing to get yourself shot."

The thermometer said he was cooler than he had been but still feverish.

David remained silent as he struggled into a sitting position.

Julianne helped prop him up against the pillows. "Well?"

"Thanks," he said with another tentative smile. "It's kind of hard to talk to you about serious things when I'm flat on my back."

"Serious things like where you've been for the past five months?" She hated that her voice was shaking, but she couldn't help it. "Like why you've let me believe you were dead all this time?"

"I realize you're upset," David said as he tried to take her hand.

Julianne jerked away from him. "Of course I'm upset. I'm worried and angry and confused, and I can't wrap my mind around any of this."

"I know."

Tears sprang to her eyes, and she dashed them away. "How did you think I'd react when you simply dropped by in the middle of the night?" She gestured toward his bandaged side. "And you have the nerve to ask me to trust you?"

"You used to," he said quietly.

"That was before you disappeared on me. I thought you were dead," Julianne reminded him. "How do you expect me to feel?"

"I understand." David took her hand, and this time he wouldn't let it go. "I hated to do it, but I didn't know any other way to protect you. Please believe me."

"So, you're telling me that breaking my heart and tearing my life to shreds was for my own good?" she snapped, trying to free her hand.

But David clung to it. "I should have taken you with me. I regretted it the minute I left, but I believed it would be safer for you." He exhaled wearily. "I was in such hot water that I thought you'd be better off without me."

"What happened?" Julianne demanded. "What kind of trouble are you in?"

He winced. "It's a long story."

"What are you talking about?"

He took a deep breath, then met her gaze.

What she saw in his eyes frightened her more than anything in her life—even more than his return from the dead with a gunshot wound.

"I've been lying to you ever since I got out of the Marines."

Julianne gasped. "You've been lying to me since before we were married?"

David wouldn't let her pull away from him. He kept holding her hand. "Please sit down for a minute. Let me explain." He had to make her understand. He had to prove that everything he'd done had been to protect her.

After a moment, she sat down on the bed beside him.

He gazed into his wife's green eyes, the ones he'd thought he'd never see again. They had always been so full of love for him. Now they were full of anger and scorn.

Even though Julianne was understandably furious with him, he was thrilled to have her beside him. He would never be able to tell her how empty he'd been without her and how glad he was to have a reason to come back.

David thought of the FBI motto: *Fidelity, Bravery, Integrity.* He was determined to show her those qualities didn't apply only to the FBI.

"I told you that I got a job with the IRS after I left the Marines," David began. "Remember how surprised you were when I decided to work there?"

She nodded.

"Well, it wasn't the IRS," he said. "It was the FBI."

"What in the world were you doing at the FBI?" Julianne asked.

"I know you've heard of Mike Fulton."

She paled. "The criminal?"

"Yes, I was part of the operation that finally got him sent to prison," he said. "I was undercover. I even got arrested when Fulton's guys did so they wouldn't suspect me. I thought I was in the clear after that."

"You told me the IRS sent you to a seminar in Ohio that week," Julianne whispered.

"Yeah, that's what I told you," David said.

She turned away and didn't respond.

There was nothing to say. He'd lied to her all along.

When Julianne faced him, he could read the obvious question in her hard eyes: *What else have you lied to me about?*

"Anyway, the bureau found out that my cover was blown," David went on. "Somebody was coming for me, and I had to disappear. They convinced me that it would be better for you if I got out of your life entirely. They told me that you'd never be safe as long as you were with me. I agreed to do what they wanted."

He was still holding her hand, and now he clutched it. "I can't tell you how sorry I am. I want you to understand that disappearing seemed like the best thing to do at the time. Once it was done, there was no going back. But I missed you. I knew it would be terrible for you, but I told myself that keeping you safe was worth it."

"It was so hard losing you and Mom in such a short time," she said.

"I'm sorry. I know how close you two were."

"We all were," Julianne said softly.

David remembered how his mother-in-law had always said he was the son she never had. He'd considered her to be his mom too, especially since he'd lost his own mother when he was a teenager. "I wanted to return to you after she died, but I found out our house burned down." His sorrow became anger. "That was when I knew they were trying to flush me out. They suspected I wasn't dead."

"It was an electrical fire," she said. "It couldn't have been arson."

He shook his head. "I had a fellow agent check it out. It was a professional job, something your average insurance guy wouldn't pick up on, but the agent could tell it was deliberate."

Julianne appeared shaken. "If you knew someone burned our house down intentionally, why didn't you come back for me? Why did you desert me?"

"I thought it was safer for both of us if I stayed dead," David answered. "Then I learned they were sending somebody after you."

"Me?" It came out in a choked whisper. "Why?"

He stared down at the bed. "That's what I was trying to find out."

"You mean this guy who shot you wants to kill me?" Julianne asked, sounding shocked.

"Nobody has to worry about him anymore." David tightened his jaw. "But it doesn't mean Fulton won't send somebody else."

Julianne glanced toward the French doors.

David followed her gaze. The curtains were partially open, and he could see the backyard and the woods beyond. It was a peaceful view. When she faced him again, he read the uncertainty in her eyes. She was obviously wondering who had been watching her.

"How could you do this to me?" she finally asked, her voice shaking. "How could you put me in this kind of danger and not even warn me about it?"

"I couldn't tell you," he said. "At least, not everything. And I didn't want to worry you."

"You didn't want to worry me?" Julianne yanked her hand out of his and jumped off the bed. "That's why you didn't tell me that we could be killed at any minute? Thanks for looking out for me."

"Please try to understand."

"This is my fault," she said, pacing the room. "I should have known that you would never be satisfied with an accounting job. You're too much of an adrenaline junkie."

"That's not fair," David said. "You act like there's something wrong with wanting to keep people safe and stop the criminals from doing whatever they want."

"So you risk your own life and everyone else's around you?" Julianne stopped pacing and put a hand over her mouth. "Are you telling me that Mom didn't die of natural causes?"

"No, don't even consider it," he said firmly. "I also checked into Mom's death, and there was no evidence of foul play. You know that she had been sick for a long time."

She sank down onto the side of the bed. "I thought you didn't reenlist in the Marines because you knew how worried I was about what might happen to you."

"I did. Sort of."

Julianne glared at him.

"At least the FBI is in the country," David reasoned. "I could have been shipped anywhere while I was in the Marines, and I knew you didn't want that."

"You pretended you had a desk job?"

"I did have a desk job." He swiped one hand across his mouth. "I hated majoring in accounting, but I figured it would always get me a job if I needed one. You remember how mad my dad was when I went into the Marines after I graduated. When my enlistment was up, I wanted us to get married, and I knew how you felt about being shipped overseas, so I started searching for accounting jobs. I applied at the IRS, and somebody from the FBI contacted me instead."

"About accounting?" she asked, raising her eyebrows.

"At the time, yes. I thought it was pretty cool."

Julianne shook her head.

"They arranged for it to seem like I was working for the IRS, and a lot of what I did was financial," David explained. "Mostly going through records that had been seized and running down money-laundering schemes. Making connections from small-time operations to their big-time bosses. It was interesting, but it wasn't dangerous—at least I never thought so. I definitely never imagined I was putting you in danger."

"And then?" she asked.

"They wanted me to go undercover," David replied. "At first, I was going to remain on the sidelines, but Fulton liked me, and my bosses decided I was too valuable to take off the job. I stayed until it was time to pull them all in for money laundering."

"You had to be there when they were arrested?"

"Actually, I did. I had to be taken into custody with the rest of Fulton's men so they wouldn't realize I was part of the setup."

"Did you even think about what would happen afterward?" Julianne asked.

"Of course I did," he said. "I used a fake name and address and changed my appearance. When everything was over, Bryan Matteson, my alter ego, would get a fairly stiff sentence for his part in the operation and end up taking his own life before he could be sent to prison. He was the one who was supposed to have his death faked, not me."

"Then what happened?"

"I don't know," David admitted. "Fulton discovered who I really was. He was in prison by then, but he's still running things with his son, Paul."

"Is Paul in prison as well?"

"No, he wasn't involved in the money-laundering part of the operation as far as we could prove," he said. "But they found out my real name, and they found out about you."

"I still don't understand why you didn't come back for me," she said.

"I desperately wanted to," David said. "It was either let you and everybody else think I was dead or wait for Fulton's men to hunt both of us down. Even if you had been willing to go on the run with me, you had your mother to take care of. She couldn't have gone with us because she was too sick. She would have been all alone, and we both know Dannie wouldn't have helped her."

Julianne bit her lip. "You're right. Mom was too fragile for any kind of stress. And Dannie wouldn't give up her home in Seattle. She doesn't know how to put someone else's needs before her own, even temporarily."

"I didn't see what else I could do," he said, putting his hand over hers. "As long as I was alive, you'd be in danger."

"Then why come back now?" she asked. "Why not stay dead and leave me alone? Then they wouldn't have any reason to come after me."

"But they're after you, whether I had come back or not," David insisted. "When I heard that, I couldn't stay dead. I couldn't let anything happen to you, not after what I've already done." He squeezed her hand. "I realize I hurt you, and I can't apologize enough. I don't want anything to happen to you because of me, and there's nothing I won't do to keep you safe."

"Are you talking about what happened to the man who shot you?"

He looked away. "I didn't have a choice."

"If he's dead, then why are they still after us?" Julianne asked.

"As soon as Fulton finds out about that guy, he'll send someone else to take care of us," David explained. "We have to get out of here before it's too late."

She pushed his hand away and stood. "I don't understand. Why would they be after me? Do they know you're still alive?"

He hesitated. "I'm not sure, but it won't be long before they figure it out."

"So, what are you going to do?" Julianne asked.

"I need to get in touch with Mack and ask him what's going on," David said, referring to Jeff Macklin, an agent he worked with at the bureau. "He'll give us the location of a safe house. Once we get there, I'll decide what to do next."

She took a step back from him. "I'm not going."

"What?"

"How did you get here?"

He frowned. "I took the bus to the street on the other side of the woods behind the house and then walked through. Why?"

"I wanted to make sure you didn't have a car somewhere," Julianne said. "I'll let you stay here until you're feeling better and you don't have a fever anymore. Then you need to move on. I don't want to be involved in any of this."

"You don't understand," he said. "You already are involved. I don't know how to explain it to you more clearly. You can't sit here and wait for Fulton to send somebody to kill you."

She crossed her arms over her chest. "How am I supposed to know if you're telling me the truth?"

"Have I ever—"

Julianne cut him off. "Don't ask me if you've ever lied to me before. Don't you dare ask me that right now. Our whole marriage seems to have been a lie. I don't know what to believe anymore."

"Please listen," David said.

"Listen to what?" she asked. "To some crazy story about you being in the FBI and faking your own death because criminals were chasing you? How do I know you didn't just get tired of me after seven years of marriage?"

"Come on," he said. "That would never happen."

"It happens," Julianne argued. "Sometimes men abandon their wives, but they don't usually pretend they've died in a tragic car crash."

"Not me," David insisted. "You know me. I wouldn't do that."

"I *thought* I knew you," Julianne said. "Dannie used to tell me that I should worry about what you were doing all those times you had to work late or go to a meeting out of town. She suspected that you were having an affair."

"What?" David asked, stunned.

"She told me it was suspicious the way you'd bring me presents every time you came home from one of your many trips," Julianne said. "And she found it strange that I couldn't get in touch with you when you were gone."

"I brought you presents because I loved you and missed you and was glad to be home again," he explained. "Until last year or so, I wasn't gone that much."

"It was still too much," she muttered.

He rubbed one hand over his mouth. "So Dannie told you I was having an affair."

"Well, she didn't say she knew it for sure," Julianne said. "She claimed it was the most likely explanation." She shook her head. "I should never tell her anything about my life. She always gives me advice, and she can never keep her mouth shut about personal things."

"Which means the whole West Coast has probably heard about my alleged philandering," David said. "Do you really believe that I would ever cheat on you?"

"Of course not," Julianne said. "I told her that her assumption was ridiculous. You were committed to me and our marriage, and once you made a promise, you kept it." She blinked hard. "I told her I knew you loved me."

"I never lied to you about how I felt," he said. "There's never been anyone else. I never lied about loving you or wanting to be married to you. I never lied about wanting to keep anything from happening to you."

"Right, you just lied to me about everything else," she snapped.

David raked one hand through his disheveled hair and sighed. "All right, I deserved that. I was completely wrong. We should have discussed it before I took the job."

"I still can't believe you didn't tell me what you were doing."

"Once I was in the undercover part of it, everything happened so fast, and there was nothing I could do," he said. "Nobody was supposed to die at the raid when we finally arrested Fulton. But some of his men knew what we were going to do, and they began shooting our agents. It wasn't part of the plan."

"I guess not," Julianne said, acid in her tone.

"I can't fix what's already done," David said. "I can only try to get us both out of the mess I've made and promise I'll do my best to never get into another one."

She said nothing.

"Please believe me," he begged. "I swear I'm telling you the truth. I understand you're furious with me and you can't trust me. If you don't want to be married to me anymore, I guess I can understand that too. But at least let me get you somewhere safe for now."

"You're not going anywhere in the shape you're in," Julianne said, the words sounding forced. "You're not much use here, and you won't go to the hospital, which is where you should be."

"We don't have time," David said. "Our lives are in danger, and we need to get to a safe house as soon as possible."

"If you want to do that, I won't try to stop you," she said. "If you want to stay until you're stronger, that's fine with me. I don't want anything to happen to you, but that doesn't mean we're going back to the way it was before you left. It's too late for that."

"All right," he said, not wanting the pain to show in his voice. He didn't think he succeeded.

"I'll fix you some breakfast," Julianne offered. "You need to eat something to get your strength back. How about a glass of orange juice to start?"

"Sure," David said, avoiding her eyes. "Thanks."

"I'll go see what else I have for you," she said. "You like ham and eggs. Maybe some toast to fill you up. Lanky as you are, you've always had a healthy appetite."

As Julianne walked by him, he wanted to stroke her hair or touch her face, so he could tell himself she was real, but her expression warned him against it.

When she was gone, David nestled into the pillows and closed his eyes, letting his body relax, feeling himself drift into darkness. Suddenly he was running down a dark, wet alley. He couldn't see anyone, but he knew they were coming for him, and he knew he had to get to Julianne before they did. If he could reach her, they'd be safe. If he could just run faster.

They were closer now. David could hear them calling him. He couldn't understand what they were saying, but he realized they wanted him to stop. They wanted him to give up.

He ran faster, his breath coming harder, but they were still there. They were behind him. Beside him. Around him. One of them touched him.

"David?"

Startled, he bolted up in bed, his eyes wide and his heart pounding. He patted the bedding around him.

Julianne froze beside him, clutching a tray of food.

He stared at her, and then he exhaled shakily. "Sorry," he murmured. "Guess I was dreaming."

"What were you trying to find?" she asked. "Your gun?"

"Yeah," David said, wiping the sweat from his lip. "I'm sorry."

Julianne didn't tell him it was okay. Instead, she set the tray on his lap and said, "Your juice is on the table next to you."

"Breakfast smells good," he said, forcing a smile. "Thank you."

"Sure." She turned to go.

"Didn't you make yourself anything?" David asked, stopping her. He wasn't ready for her to leave.

"It's in the kitchen," she said.

"Do you think you could come in here to eat?" He shrugged. "Maybe we could talk."

For a moment, he thought he saw love and longing in her eyes, but then her expression hardened.

"I've already said everything I have to say." Julianne dropped her gaze and sighed. "I don't know what to do. I don't know what to think."

"I can't stand the thought of you sitting on the other side of the house and not being able to see you," David said. "It's been such a long time, and I've missed you so much."

She paused, evidently debating his request. "I'll be right back."

Julianne returned with her breakfast on a tray and set it down on the bed beside him. Then she pulled a chair up close, and for a few minutes they ate in silence.

"Tell me about Mom," David said finally.

"It broke her heart when she thought you were dead," she said, the grief in her eyes still fresh. "She loved you."

"I loved her too, and I feel terrible that I wasn't there for her." He felt his throat tighten, and he took a long time chewing a bite of ham. "But I figured losing me was better than her losing both of us."

Julianne stared at her plate, pushing around a piece of egg without actually spearing it with her fork. "So I had to lose both you and her."

"I'm really sorry she's gone," David continued. "And I'm sorry I wasn't with you. I realize it was rough on you, dealing with everything alone."

"I had my sister," she said, a touch of sarcasm in her voice.

He laughed softly. "Yeah."

Julianne studied him for a moment. "I don't know why this Mike Fulton would be after me. If he found out you're not dead, why isn't he after you? Why would he care about me?"

"I'm not sure," David admitted. "Maybe he wants to get back at me for what happened or force me out of hiding."

"Wasn't burning down our house enough?" she asked, her voice cracking.

"I guess not." He set his fork down and pushed his half-eaten breakfast aside. "Do you want to talk about the fire?"

"Fortunately, I wasn't there when it happened, so I didn't get hurt," Julianne said. "When I received frantic calls from our neighbors, I rushed home. By the time I arrived, the house was already gone."

"I'm so sorry," David said quietly. How could he ever apologize enough for everything he'd put her through?

"It was devastating. Everything we owned—everything I had to remember you by—was burned in the fire. The mementos Mom left me and our family pictures were lost."

He winced. "What about your artwork?"

"All of it was destroyed," she said. "The only things left were the clothes on my back and my car."

"I'm sorry that you weren't able to salvage anything," David told her.

"I have our wedding portrait that was Mom's," Julianne said. "They gave me a box of things from your office. It was in the trunk of my car when the house burned."

"What was in it?" he asked, suddenly tense.

"Not much. Your mug and that picture of me sitting under a tree. And a notebook."

David narrowed his eyes. "What notebook?"

"A notebook with mostly numbers and initials," she replied. "It's in your handwriting. Do you want to see it later?"

"I want to see it now."

Julianne put her hand on David's shoulder, stopping him from getting out of bed. "You need to rest and finish your breakfast."

"I need to see the notebook," David insisted. "This might involve more than revenge. Maybe whatever's in that notebook is something they want. If they want it, that means it's important."

"If it's so important, then why would somebody at your office give it to me in the first place?" she asked.

"It could have been somebody who wasn't paying attention," he reasoned. "Somebody who didn't know what it was. I can't even guess unless I see it."

"It can't wait another five minutes?" Julianne asked.

"No, it can't," David said, struggling to get up.

"Okay, I'll get the notebook and bring it to you," she relented. "You finish eating."

Julianne retrieved the notebook from her office and carried it to the bedroom. David's plate and glass were empty. At least he still had an appetite. She set the dishes to one side and handed the notebook to him.

David flipped through the pages, shaking his head. "This is mine, but it has nothing to do with Fulton or any other case."

"Then what is it?" she asked.

He gave her a mischievous grin, and his face reddened slightly. "It's part of a puzzle I was solving on a video game."

"What?" Julianne asked.

"It was an incredibly complicated maze," David said. "I was trying to figure out how to get through it alive and not be killed the minute I got to the other side."

She gaped at him, unable to believe what she was hearing. "This is about a video game?"

"Sometimes when I was out of town, had downtime, and couldn't be seen by anybody, I played this game to pass the time," he answered. "Is there something wrong with that?"

"Do you realize how ridiculous this is?" Julianne asked.

"It's dead serious," David said, his gray eyes flashing. "Just because Fulton isn't after this notebook doesn't mean we're not in danger. He's still going to try to kill us both."

"How do I know this isn't something you're making up?"

"Do you really believe that I shot myself as a joke or something?" he asked.

"No," she admitted. "I don't know what to think."

"Let me get you somewhere safe," David said. "Then if you don't want to see me again, I'll respect your decision."

Was that what she wanted? For five months, Julianne had been wishing for nothing more than to see David one more time, so she could tell him how much she loved him and apologize for not kissing him goodbye the last time he left.

Right now, Julianne wanted to tell him to get out of her house and never come back. She wanted to bury herself in his arms and cry. But she didn't do either. Instead, she wrapped her arms around herself and walked over to the French doors, gazing out into the woods that didn't seem nearly as ominous as they had last night in the dark.

"I don't know if things can ever be the way they were," she said, watching his reflection in the glass, realizing what she would have given only twenty-four hours ago to see him. "Too much has happened."

"I told you I'd respect whatever decision you make about our relationship," David said, his voice soft.

Julianne was hurt that he wasn't arguing with her, but it was foolish to feel that way. David was the kind of man who said what he thought and left it at that. He didn't care who agreed with him. He didn't care who believed him. He was simply who he was.

At least she'd thought so.

Please, God, what am I supposed to do? How can I believe anything he tells me ever again?

"For months, you let me think you were dead," Julianne said. "Only hours ago, I found out that you're alive. You can't expect me to flip my emotions on and off."

"I don't," he said, the tenderness in his voice sending a deep ache into her heart. "I just want you to—"

The doorbell rang.

Julianne froze at the sound of the doorbell.

"Where's my gun?" David whispered.

She motioned toward the closet. "Top shelf."

He struggled to get up.

"No, stay put." Julianne rushed over to the closet, opened the door, and retrieved the gun.

The doorbell rang again.

"Fulton's men wouldn't be ringing the doorbell," he said. "Are you expecting anybody?"

She shook her head as she handed him the weapon.

The visitor knocked on the door.

"Okay," David said, his breathing a little more rapid than usual. "I want you to check the peephole without making a sound. If it's not somebody you know, get back in here with me. If it is, say you're sick and get rid of whoever it is. All right?"

The knocking continued.

Her heart pounded, but she nodded. Then she took a deep breath and went to the door.

It was Larry.

Julianne stifled a sigh of relief. She ran her hands through her hair, messing it up, and opened the door.

Larry gaped at her from behind his thick glasses. "Mother was worried about you when we didn't see you go to work, so she thought you might like this." He thrust a casserole dish covered in aluminum foil toward her.

"How nice," she said, accepting the dish. "Tell your mom thanks."

"She wanted me to tell you that it came out of the freezer, so you'll have to let it thaw first, but you shouldn't put it on the counter because it might spoil."

Julianne blinked at him. "I'll do that."

"I probably should take that for you," he said. "To the kitchen, I mean. Frozen and all, it's kind of heavy."

She had no choice but to usher him to the kitchen. It was a mess from her cooking breakfast, but at least the two sets of dirty dishes were in the bedroom.

"So, are you sick or what?" Larry asked.

"Yeah, I had a bad night and ended up calling in sick. I think it might be food poisoning." Julianne opened the refrigerator door for him. "But I should be better soon."

He set the casserole on a shelf in the fridge.

She closed the refrigerator and steered him toward the front door. "Tell your mom how much I appreciate her sending the casserole over."

"I will," Larry said. "She made a bunch of them last week. I'm not sure what she calls it, but it contains hamburger and vegetables. She thought you might need something to get your strength back."

"That's very kind of her," Julianne said, quickening her step.

Larry gawked at everything in the house, and she was glad David hadn't been anywhere but in the bedroom. She didn't need Larry telling his mother, who no doubt would gossip to the entire neighborhood that Julianne had a guest.

At the front door, Larry stopped and turned toward her, his dark eyes wide and earnest. "Mother said she could come over if you need somebody to help. Of course, I'd have to push her over here in her chair, but she'd be glad to sit with you if you need her."

"That's so sweet, but I'll be fine," Julianne said, opening the door.

"I'm going to take it easy today. If I feel up to it, I'll eat some of the casserole."

"I'm home all day with my telemarketing job," Larry said. "So if you need anything, give me a call. But be sure to call my mother's line."

She nodded. "Because yours is tied up when you're working. I remember."

"Right." Larry walked out the door, but he hesitated on the porch.

Standing in the open doorway, Julianne hugged herself as if she felt cold. "I'd better go. I don't want to get a chill."

"I'll tell Mother what you said." He waved, then trudged across the lawn to his house.

She closed and locked the door, then glanced around the house. All the living room curtains were drawn, and so were the ones in the kitchen and dining room. Larry couldn't have seen anything. Hopefully, no one knew there was anyone else here.

Julianne hurried to the bedroom to tell David it was only the guy from next door, but when she went inside, the bed was empty, his folded clothes were gone, and all but one set of dishes had vanished.

Had he left again?

Before she even had time to feel upset, David pushed the door closed and stepped out from behind it, fully dressed.

She caught her breath. "What are you doing?"

"I was waiting in case he came in here."

"I wasn't going to let him," Julianne said, tugging his arm. "Now get back in bed before you fall down."

"I'm not that bad off," David protested, but he sat down on the bed. "In fact, now that I've eaten, I'm feeling a lot better. So, tell me about this guy."

"Why?" she asked as she pressed her palm to his forehead. "Jealous?"

"As a matter of fact, I am," he said. "Seriously, who is he?"

"Larry Spielmann, my next-door neighbor," Julianne answered. "He's thirty-seven, and he works at home as a telemarketer. He lives with his mother, Rhoda Spielmann, and she sent over a casserole."

"Yeah, I heard."

"Actually, I'm glad Larry dropped off the casserole," she told him. "It's exactly what you need to build up your strength, and it saves me from going out for groceries and leaving you to fend for yourself."

"Neither of us needs to be left alone, and we can't stay here. If Fulton is sending someone after you, this is the first place he'll check."

"I already told you that I'm not running with you." Julianne spread the covers over him and encouraged him to drink some water. "You don't seem as hot as you were, but we need to change the bandage." She walked into the bathroom.

"Come on," he called after her. "Please reconsider."

Julianne gathered the first aid supplies, then carried them to the bedroom. "It's time to clean and bandage the wound," she said stiffly.

David pulled up his shirt on the left side, and she swabbed the area with alcohol.

"You don't understand how serious this is," he said through clenched teeth.

"You don't understand how serious *this* is," she said, gesturing at the wound. "You should have it examined by somebody who knows what he's doing. You need stitches."

David groaned when she poured on more alcohol.

Julianne blotted his skin dry and taped two pads of gauze over the front and back of the wound. Then she pulled his shirt down and covered him with a blanket. "I don't have much in the way of painkillers besides ibuprofen. I'll get it for you if you want."

"We have to talk about this."

"I'll bring you another glass of orange juice too," she said, ignoring his comment. "You need it. Do you want the ibuprofen or not?"

"Forget all that for a moment," David said. "We need to talk."

Julianne pressed her lips together so they wouldn't tremble. "I'll get your juice." Before he could say anything else, she hurried out of the room.

When Julianne returned with a glass of orange juice and a bottle of ibuprofen, David didn't insist they have a conversation about their situation. He merely thanked her.

He swallowed a couple of pills and drank the juice. "I guess I'd better get some more sleep."

"What about that?" she asked, pointing at the gun beside him on the bed. "Isn't it dangerous for you to keep it right there?"

"It's okay. It's not going to go off unless I want it to." David stared at her, concern in his gray eyes. "I'm not trying to scare you, but if somebody shows up searching for us, I want it close at hand."

He was definitely scaring her, but how could she be certain that all this was nothing but an elaborate trick? Just like his death?

"I'll get the lights," she told him. "Call me if you need anything."

David settled down into the bed and closed his eyes.

Julianne watched him for a moment, remembering how often she had begged God for this moment, to see David alive and at home, to have another chance to tell him how much she loved him and how glad she was to be his wife. Now she had exactly what she'd prayed for. Or did she?

She switched off the lights and shut the door.

Davidd slept fitfully most of the day.

At some point, Julianne woke him up to take his temperature. She also encouraged him to eat a bowl of her neighbor's casserole. After he finished, he quickly fell back into oblivion.

When Julianne woke him the next morning, she was dressed and had already made breakfast. She set two trays of scrambled eggs, toast, and bacon on the nightstand.

David felt uncomfortably hot and exhausted, and he was afraid that he couldn't do much to protect her if he had to. He winced when she examined the wound. It was still red and swollen and warm to the touch.

"It's okay," he told her, dutifully taking a swallow of milk with the ibuprofen she gave him. "It's healing."

"You should have stitches," Julianne said again.

"It might not be pretty, but it'll heal," David assured her. "I've seen it before."

She crossed her arms over her chest. "Something else you didn't tell me about?"

He gave her a weary grin and started eating his eggs. "A couple of my friends in the Marines got shot. Both times I had to help get them back to get patched up. Last year one of the agents came into the office and passed out in front of my desk. He was shot in the stomach, so it was bad. I was afraid he was going to die right there. He's fine now."

"Because he went to the hospital, didn't he?"

David shrugged.

Julianne sat in a chair. She stared at him for a moment, then blurted out, "I can't deal with any of this. I'm not sure I can ever trust you again. If you think you need to go, then you should leave. But don't include me in your plans."

"I can't let you stay here and be killed," David responded evenly. "If I wanted to do that, I would have remained dead. Don't you think I know what I did to you? Walking away from you was the hardest thing I've ever done in my entire life."

Her jaw clenched, and she turned away.

"It's been awful without you, but I thought you'd be safe when I left," he continued. "Now I'm sure you're in danger. Officially, I'm dead, and I have connections. I could get out of the country if I needed to. But that would mean leaving you defenseless. I won't do that. And if you refuse to go with me, then all I can do is stay here and try to protect you the best I can."

When Julianne faced him, David held her gaze, hoping she could see the sincerity and urgency in his eyes. She had to understand how serious this was. Going to the hospital, especially to treat a gunshot wound, would be too dangerous. But he had to admit that he wasn't strong enough to go anywhere at the moment. If they were extremely careful, they might be safe in her house for a little while longer. But he had to get her out soon.

"I'm not saying I believe any of this or that I'll do it," she responded. "But what exactly do you want me to do?"

"Go to a safe house with me," he said. "While we're there, I'll get in touch with Mack and see if he can determine Fulton's plans for us. I realize it's going to take a lot to get you to trust me again, but there's nothing I can do to make you believe me if you get killed in the next day or two. Please let me take you somewhere safe."

"I don't know. I can't—"

The doorbell rang.

Julianne whirled around, surprise in her eyes.

David grabbed the gun that was still beside him in the bed and put one finger over his lips.

She picked up her breakfast tray and slid it into a dresser drawer, food and all.

He got out of bed, gun ready. "Go on and see," he whispered when the doorbell rang again.

"I'm sure it's nothing," Julianne answered softly. "It's probably Larry checking on me. Maybe his mother is with him this time."

David clutched the gun in both hands, one finger on the trigger, and followed her down the hallway. A slatted black lacquer folding screen stood in the corner of the living room. He slipped behind it, so he could remain hidden and still see and hear everything.

Julianne opened the door. "Jim," she said, putting her hand to her disheveled hair. "I'm sorry. I'm not dressed for company, especially not my boss. I should have called in sick again."

David couldn't get a glimpse of the visitor because Julianne was blocking the doorway.

When she stepped back and the man moved closer, David tightened his grip on the gun, forcing himself to stay where he was. That was her boss? She called him Jim, but his name was Ray Gist. He worked for Fulton, so they were definitely keeping tabs on her.

David put the muzzle of the gun right above the middle hinge of the screen, training it on the man, not wanting to give himself away if he didn't have to. He prepared to shoot if Ray made a single suspicious move.

Ray gave her an apologetic smile. "I suppose I should have called, but I have to see a client nearby, so I thought I'd stop by. Are you all right? You seem to be over the worst of the food poisoning."

"Yes, I think I am. Today I'm feeling a little worn-out," Julianne said, remaining admirably cool. Nothing in her voice or expression indicated that she had an on-the-run husband hiding in her home, recuperating from being shot and claiming there were criminals after her.

She motioned to the living room. "Won't you come in for a minute? I don't want to keep you standing on the porch."

"Thanks," he said, stepping through the door. "I hate to be a bother, but it's company policy."

"What's company policy?" Julianne asked.

"Even though you said it was food poisoning, I don't want anybody at the office catching something from you, so I'm glad you stayed home," Ray said. "But if you're sick for more than three days, you'll need a doctor's note to continue getting sick pay."

"I didn't know that. I'm sorry." Her face reddened slightly. "If I can't come in tomorrow, I'll see my doctor first thing. I'm not sure what I ate, but I promise I'm not contagious. I never ran a fever or anything."

He nodded, the overhead light making his nearly bald head shine. "My apologies for dropping in on you. Is there anything I can get for you while I'm out this way?"

"I appreciate it, but no," Julianne said. "I'm sorry I didn't call and tell you I wouldn't be in again. I guess my brain isn't ready to think about work quite yet."

"It's fine. Don't worry about it." Ray gave her a fatherly pat on the shoulder. "Get some rest, and feel better."

"Thanks," she said, walking him to the door. "See you soon."

After the rumble of his car engine faded into the distance, Julianne shut and locked the door.

David emerged from behind the screen. "That's your boss? Jim something?"

She nodded. "Jim Webber."

"Tell me what you do for him," he said, trying to remain calm.

"I'm his administrative assistant."

"What exactly do you do?" David asked.

"Secretarial things," Julianne said. "Like running errands, keeping his schedule, filing papers, and answering the phone. I basically help out wherever he needs me." She tilted her head. "Why?"

"What does he pay you?"

When she told him, David was stunned. "He pays you that much for being a secretary?"

She pursed her lips. "Well, I thought it was pretty high, but Jim said I'd be training for something better soon and he didn't want me to get away before then."

"I'll bet he didn't want you to get away," he muttered.

"What do you mean?"

"That's Ray Gist, not Jim Webber," David explained. "He works for Fulton's son. Ray was overseeing the bookkeeping on some of Paul's bigger operations, but I guess they figured he had the right look to play the part of a kindly boss."

"Are you crazy?" Julianne asked, sounding shocked. "He's simply a nice guy. In fact, he reminds me of my dad."

"Most of the people who want to kill you are dads," David said. "Ray has three daughters and eight grandchildren. He coaches Little League in his neighborhood and volunteers at the soup kitchen downtown."

"What about the company I work for?" she asked. "I've never noticed anything even remotely illegal."

"It's probably one of the fronts for their money-laundering operation."

"All right, I believe you." Julianne glared at him, but he could see the fear behind the scowl.

"How did you find out about the job in the first place?" he asked. "An ad? An agency?"

"No." She glanced up at the ceiling, breathing out hard. "It was through my real estate agent."

"You didn't think it was a little strange for your real estate agent to tell you about a job opportunity?" David asked.

"Not at all," Julianne said. "We went to school together, and she was a friend of mine. I mentioned that I was worried about finding a good job, and she told me about this opening."

"What did she tell you about the job?" he asked.

"She said a friend of hers recently had a baby, and she changed her mind about returning to work," she replied. "The woman's boss needed someone to take over her position right away."

"What made you apply for it?"

"I don't know," Julianne admitted. "I didn't have much work experience after spending the last seven years trying to be an artist, and I was sure I wouldn't get hired. But Jim was nice, and he said he'd train me." She shrugged. "I guess I didn't question it because I desperately needed something good to happen to me."

David was alarmed by the way Fulton's people had gotten close to Julianne. Unfortunately, he knew that their reach extended beyond her new job. "What about this house?"

Julianne shook her head and covered her face with both hands. "My agent said the seller had suddenly been transferred and needed to move as soon as possible. She claimed it had just gone on the market, and she urged me to snap it up before someone else did."

She told him what she'd paid for the house, which happened to be most of her insurance money from the fire, with just enough left for her to get started on rebuilding her life.

"I can't believe that was a setup too," Julianne moaned. "I thought

I could trust her, and they paid her off to get me to take this job and house?"

"It seems like it." David went over to her and rested his hand on her shoulder. "I'm sorry. You've had more than your fair share of trouble and deceit. But you've got to believe me now. I'm going to do everything I possibly can to get us both out of this."

"Do they know you're here?" she asked.

"I don't think they realize it yet," he said. "If they do anything to you before they're sure I'm here, they'll lose their bait, so they're waiting and watching. We have to get out of here before they discover we've already reconnected."

Julianne frowned. "So, I go into hiding with you or stay and get killed."

"At this point, those are your only choices."

Julianne spent the day with the lights low and the curtains drawn. She didn't even walk outside to collect the mail. When it got late, she heated up more of Rhoda's casserole for herself and her patient.

David had slept most of the day, and she had to wake him to eat. She sat in the chair by his bed, both of them with a tray of food, and he told her about what he'd been doing since his supposed car accident.

"Mostly keeping my head down," he admitted as he ate. "I've been working on a lot of different cases, trying to track down evidence that certain organizations have a criminal connection. It was pretty much what I was doing before I had to disappear, but I was working somewhere we believed they wouldn't find me. At least not too quickly."

"Where was that?" Julianne asked.

David swallowed a forkful of casserole. "I've been working as an accountant for a large oil company in Houston. The department's so big that we figured nobody would even notice me."

She frowned, puzzled. "But I thought you were still working for the FBI."

"I was. I am."

"Then how did you keep up with your accounting job too?" Julianne asked.

"I did enough to know what was going on," he replied. "But I sent most of it through a private connection to a group that works for the bureau. They had several people doing the grunt work for me. They didn't do it perfectly or too quickly. I didn't want to come across like some whiz kid or stand out in any way. They'd send it back, and I'd make sure it got to where it was supposed to go. Mainly I kept a low profile and tried to appear busy."

"So, you were doing the same kind of work for the bureau that you'd been doing before you went undercover, right?"

David nodded. "I was doing bookwork and reporting my findings for other agents to investigate. Maybe I am an adrenaline junkie like you said, but I left the Marines and took that mostly safe job with the bureau because of you."

"Because of me?" she asked, incredulous. "I didn't tell you to take that job with the FBI. I wasn't even aware of what you were doing."

"I accepted the job because you were more important to me than getting my fix of action and adventure," he said. "And you're the reason why I came back. I don't want anything to happen to you. Please come with me somewhere safe. Is this place so important to you? More important than your life?"

"No, I don't care about this house," Julianne said. "It's not home. I don't think it ever will be. If what you say is true, it's a setup anyway, just like my job. But you're asking me to take off with you and hide out somewhere I know nothing about. Even if I go with you, what happens next? How long will it last? Do we run for the rest of our lives? Or do you ditch me somewhere and disappear again?"

"I can't answer those questions," David said, his eyes fixed on hers. "Except for the last one. I'm not leaving you again unless you tell me to go. And then you're going to have to be very convincing for me to believe you."

For the longest moment, Julianne was caught in the truth and intensity of his eyes. Then she put down her fork, got out of the chair, and carefully peeked around the curtains and out toward the woods.

Fulton and his men had set it up for her to be here in this particular house. Were they watching them now?

"I moved into this house a month ago," she said, carefully wiping the fear and uncertainty from her expression. "They could have killed me anytime. They could have waited until I was home and burned me up with the house, like they burned our old one. I don't understand why we have to go on the run right now."

"I can't hide here forever," he said. "If they don't already know where I am, they will soon. Unless you want them to realize something's going on, you'll have to go back to work eventually. The longer it goes on, the more likely one of us will make a mistake, and in our situation, mistakes are fatal."

Julianne didn't say anything for a few seconds, and then she put her hand on his forehead. "I'm trying to tell if you're still feverish. Even if I agree to go with you, it won't do either of us any good if you pass out on the way."

"I'm fine," David muttered, finishing the last of his food.

"I think you're better," she admitted, "but I'm not sure if you're okay. Maybe you should take a hot bath and soak for a while."

He shook his head. "Bad idea. I don't need the bathwater getting into the wound. I'd do better with a shower, if that's all right with you. While I'm in there, I want you to stay alert. Keep the curtains drawn, and don't answer the door for anybody, not even your next-door neighbor."

"I promise," Julianne said as she helped him to his feet. She noticed he carried his gun into the bathroom, but maybe that was for the best.

Julianne didn't feel comfortable being too far away while he showered. She tried to convince herself that she stayed in case he got light-headed or needed something. But the truth was that she was scared. Julianne was vulnerable while David was taking a shower, and she had no way to protect herself. David had always wanted to teach her how to use a gun, but she had refused, saying she'd let him be in charge of home security. Now she wished she had accepted his offer.

She reflected on his repeated pleas to take her somewhere safe. Why did she continue to refuse? What was wrong with her?

But she knew what was wrong. No matter how sincere he seemed when he made promises to never abandon her again, she couldn't help but question if she could really trust him after what he had put her through.

David seemed steadier and more awake when he returned to the bedroom, but he was still pale, and his wet hair was almost black against his skin. He'd had no choice but to dress in the only clothes he had.

"I'll go buy you some new clothes," Julianne offered. "At least socks and underwear."

He shook his head, and a trickle of water ran down his neck from his hair to the towel draped around his shoulders. "That would be the worst thing you could do. You might as well tell Paul Fulton I'm here and ask if he'd please send someone over."

He was right, of course. They already had a reason to suspect he was here since Julianne wasn't going to work, so if she bought men's clothing, it would be a dead giveaway. She briefly considered borrowing a few things from next door, but that was a ridiculous idea. David was lean, but he was muscular and well-built. Larry was a little shorter than David and almost painfully thin. David would never be able to squeeze himself into any of Larry's clothes.

"It's all right," David said, giving her a wry smile. "I'll pick up some things once we're out of here."

"If we go," she said. "You still haven't told me what your plan is."

"You're supposed to go back to work in the morning or call in sick, right?" he asked.

Julianne nodded.

"So, nobody would think it was strange if you pulled out of the garage at your usual time and headed toward the office like you do on any other workday."

"Probably not," she said. "But what if they have somebody follow me? If all this is a setup, they must be keeping an eye on me."

David ran his fingers through his wet hair. "It's extremely likely that they'll follow you if they think I'm headed this way, but I'm afraid it's a chance we'll have to take. Maybe they'll be satisfied that you're heading toward the office because they can watch you there. They might even search the house while you're gone."

"I've wondered if someone has been in my house," Julianne said. "There have been times when I've come home and found things a bit off. Nothing I'm sure about, just a feeling that something wasn't exactly where I put it before I left that day."

"I wouldn't be surprised if they were rummaging around for evidence that we'd been in touch," he said gravely.

"Let's say they don't follow me to work tomorrow morning," she said. "What happens when I don't show up at the office?"

"They'll wait a little while to see if you're simply late," David said. "When they realize you're not coming, they'll send somebody after you. By then, we'll have had time to get out of town. How long does it take you to get to work most days?"

"Between thirty and forty-five minutes," Julianne replied. "It depends on traffic."

"That's not much of a start, but at least it's something," he said. "To gain some extra time, we'll get going a bit early, and you can hang some clothes up where they're noticeable in the back window. If anybody is watching, he'll think you're dropping things off at the dry cleaner's before work."

"What about you?"

"I'll ride in the trunk."

She cringed. "Then what?"

"I need to get a burner phone," David said. "We can't use yours, and mine was destroyed after Farrar's bullet hit it."

His comment about the shooting reminded Julianne of the bruises on his hands and his face. She glanced at them. They were just as vivid as when he'd arrived. "Farrar's the guy who shot you?"

He nodded. "My phone kept him from hitting anything important."

"And he's dead now," she said, feeling sick. It was still so difficult to wrap her mind around the entire terrifying situation.

"Yes, and I had to dump the phone in the lake," David said. "I couldn't have whoever found him trace it back to me."

"You?" Julianne asked. "Or whoever you were pretending to be at the moment?"

"I was Bryan Matteson," he said. "I thought it was unlikely they could connect me to you by that name, but they figured it out. I heard a rumor that there's a leak in the unit I was in at the bureau. It could explain how they found out I was alive. Anyway, getting a burner phone shouldn't be any trouble."

"Fine," Julianne said, trying to take it all in. A horrible thought popped into her mind. "Do I even know your real name?"

"David Cooper Montgomery, as I always told you. Honestly." He gently put both hands on her shoulders. "Just like it says on our marriage license."

"And on your death certificate," she added.

David dropped his hands. "I realize this has been extremely hard on you. I know I hurt you with what I did, but that's not why I did it. I would never intentionally do anything to hurt you."

"I'm sorry," Julianne whispered. "I'm angry and confused and scared. But that doesn't give me permission to be cruel."

"It's all right," he said, putting his arms around her. "Everything's all right."

She rested her head against his chest, thinking of how much she had missed her husband and how right it felt to be in his arms. She felt warm, cherished, and safe. Was it a memory or an illusion? Had it ever been real?

"I didn't mean to snap at you," Julianne murmured into his shirt, wondering if he could understand the words or even hear them. "I used to snap at you sometimes, didn't I? I shouldn't have. Maybe I made it easy for you to leave."

David pulled back and turned her face up to his. "No, that's not true at all. Leaving you was the hardest thing I've ever done."

She stood there for a moment longer, trembling in his arms, then shrugged away from him. "So, what do we do after we get out of Springfield?"

"Like I said before, I need to get in touch with Mack," he answered. "He'll direct us to a safe house, and we'll stay there until he lets us know what to do next. I'm sorry I can't tell you more than that, but if we don't have details yet, there's no chance anybody else will find out."

"All right, I'll go," Julianne said, glancing around the bedroom.

David searched her eyes. "Really?"

She swallowed hard and nodded.

David tried to get Julianne to sleep in the bed that night and let him take the sofa, but he was still pale, and she knew with his long frame that he would never get comfortable enough on the couch to actually rest. She made him drink more orange juice with his ibuprofen and finally urged him to settle into bed for the night.

Julianne said a silent prayer as she pressed her hand to his forehead to see if he had a fever. He still had one, but it wasn't very high.

"Go to sleep," she said, tugging the covers up to his shoulders. "Call me if you need anything."

David patted the gun beside his pillow. "You do the same."

She carried her toiletries into the guest bathroom and stood before the sink, washing her face and trying not to think about what was going to happen tomorrow. She'd never been the adventurous sort. How she'd ended up marrying a guy like David she'd never know. It was people like him who settled distant lands, sailed into uncharted waters, and went to the moon.

"If it had been up to me," Julianne had told him once, "I would still be sitting in my cave, warning everybody how dangerous fire is."

"It takes both kinds of people," David had replied. "Somebody needs to stand back and wonder if a grand new idea is actually practical, then scrape up the pieces when it fails spectacularly." He'd hugged her tightly. "That's one of the reasons why we're so great together."

She rinsed her face and blotted it dry. Maybe it was true. But in the morning they were heading into something completely foreign to her. What good would she be to David then? What good was it going to do either of them if she stepped out into whatever he was leading them into and didn't trust him?

As Julianne brushed her teeth, she thought again about going to the police, but she knew that would be dangerous. Fulton could have his people planted anywhere. David seemed to think so at least. Trusting the local law could get them both killed. Not trusting David could get them both killed. If she wasn't sure about him, she shouldn't go at all. But what alternative did she have?

She put on her pajamas and got into her makeshift bed on the couch, but she couldn't fall asleep. She was about to run away from everything she knew and everything she had. But what did she have anymore except this house that she'd been manipulated into buying and a job she'd been given only so she could be watched? The car, she reminded herself. She had her Honda Accord and the miscellaneous stuff in the trunk. None of it was worth dying for.

"Please, God, help me," she whispered into the darkness. "I know I'm supposed to be strong and never afraid. But I'm not strong, and I am afraid. Show me what I should do. If I need to stay, show me. If I need to go, show me that. Help me do whatever it is I need to do to get us out of this. And please watch over us. Amen."

Julianne rolled over to her side and a moment later flipped to her other side. Then she stretched out on her back, thinking. "Thank You that David's not dead," she added softly.

She must have fallen asleep, because the next thing she knew, someone pressed a hand over her mouth. Her eyes flew open, but she didn't dare move.

It was David.

She pushed his hand away and pressed her trembling lips together.

"There's somebody outside," he whispered. "Don't make a sound."

"Don't move," David murmured to Julianne. In the darkness, he could hardly see her shadow on the sofa.

She did as he instructed, remaining silent and motionless.

He crossed from the couch to the front door and pulled back the curtain, allowing in a sliver of moonlight that was there and then gone. Without a sound, he moved from the living room to the dining room and then to the kitchen, barely pushing aside the curtains in each window to check if anyone was still out there.

David returned to Julianne. She hadn't left the sofa, but he noticed her hands, white in the near blackness, clutching the blanket draped over her.

"He's gone," David said. "I don't know if he was attempting to break in or if he was only peeking inside. Either way, we can't take any more chances. We've got to get out of here soon."

"If we leave in the middle of the night," she whispered, "whoever it is will know."

"That's true," he said. "Unless something else happens, we have to stick to the plan. We'll go first thing in the morning. Until then, I want you to sleep in the bedroom."

"Where will you sleep?" Julianne asked.

"In the bedroom."

"I'd rather stay here," she said. "Whoever was out there is already gone."

"I can't protect you if you're half a house away," David said. "I'll sleep on the floor and keep a distance of five feet between us at all times if you want. Just please go to the bedroom."

She got up, gathering her bedding with her.

He took her arm and guided her into the bedroom. Even with the curtains drawn over the French doors, it was slightly lighter in here. "Does your neighbor always keep her back porch light on?"

"Yes, most of the time," Julianne replied. "Rhoda is worried about prowlers, though she's never seen one."

"Give me your sheets and blanket," he said. "I'll use them on the floor. There's no point tearing up the bed now. Try to get some sleep. We have to get going early in the morning."

She glanced at the alarm clock on the nightstand, and David did too. It was 3:12.

"We don't have much more time to sleep," she told him. "So there's no use in either of us being uncomfortable. Go ahead and sleep where you were, and I'll sleep on the other side of the bed."

"If you're sure," he said.

Julianne was silent for a moment, then nodded. She curled up in the blanket and sheets she'd brought from the couch and looked expectantly at him.

Instead of stretching out on the other side of the bed, David walked over to the French doors and peered outside.

After a few minutes, he realized she was asleep.

But he had no intention of sleeping too. David feared that one of Fulton's men would return.

And he would be ready for him.

David woke Julianne at dawn before her alarm went off. "It's time to get up."

"Did you get any more sleep?" she asked.

"No, but it's okay," he said. "Are you hungry? I made breakfast."

"I'm starving," Julianne said.

David ushered her to the kitchen and pulled out a chair for her at the table. He had already prepared two plates of scrambled eggs and toast, and he'd sliced a couple of the apples that he'd found in the refrigerator. "Dig in."

Julianne buttered her toast and took a bite.

He poured two cups of coffee and prepared hers with cream and no sugar, exactly the way she liked it. After handing her the cup, he sat down next to her with his own coffee.

"Thanks," she said.

"I packed a bag of supplies and nonperishable food and stowed it in the trunk of your car," David said. "I also hung a few of your dresses in the window so they'll be visible."

"What should I pack?"

"Just the necessities," he answered, then took a sip of his coffee. "You can make a pile of the things you want to take, and I'll pack everything for you while you're in the shower."

"What else do we need to do?" Julianne asked.

David didn't want to scare her, but he had to make sure she realized how urgent this was. Watching her closely, he said, "I'll toss the extra sheets and blankets in the laundry basket with everything else and put the couch pillows back where they were. We don't want the house too neat, so it seems like you've gone to work for the day."

She gave him a wary look, then nodded.

"Be sure to return everything to their usual spots," he added. "If they realize you're gone and check the place out, I don't want them to discover any sign that I've ever been here."

"I moved some toiletries into the guest bathroom, but I'll take them back to the master bath."

Once they'd finished their food and left out enough dirty dishes for one person, Julianne transferred the toiletries, then rummaged through her dresser drawers and closet. She piled clothes and other necessities onto the bed.

"Do you have a bag?" David asked.

She retrieved a suitcase from the top shelf in the closet and handed it to him.

"When you get ready, put on an outfit that you would wear to work," he said.

While Julianne was taking a shower, David packed her suitcase, then walked through the house, making sure nothing appeared suspicious.

Julianne emerged from the bathroom with her hair and makeup done. She wore a dress and heels as if she were going to the office.

The phone rang.

She glanced at him. "Should I answer it?"

David nodded, and she took the call.

"It's Rhoda. I'm sorry to bother you so early, especially since you've been sick on top of everything else that you've had to go through, but I couldn't wait any longer."

He could hear the older woman's strident voice clearly. It was high and quavery.

"I'm feeling better today, and there's no need to apologize," Julianne said. "Is something wrong?"

"I thought you should know about Buttons," Rhoda said. "She woke me up very early, and I could tell she was sick."

"Oh no," Julianne said. "What's wrong with her?"

"I can't help thinking someone gave her something poisonous to eat," Rhoda said, her voice cracking.

"Poisonous?" Julianne gasped, staring at David.

He inched closer, trying to hear the other side of the conversation better.

"You need to get her to the vet immediately," Julianne told Rhoda. "I realize you can't do it yourself, but—"

"Larry already took her to the emergency vet," Rhoda said, interrupting her. "It was about four this morning. The bill was outrageous, of course, but we had to take her. She's my baby."

"What did the vet say?" Julianne asked.

"He says she'll be fine, thank goodness," Rhoda answered. "But I can't imagine who would have done such a horrible thing to her."

"I have no idea," Julianne said. "She's a wonderful dog."

"Did you see anybody prowling around the yard or out in the woods or anything last night?" Rhoda asked. "This is so upsetting."

"I think I heard someone outside last night," Julianne said. "But I never saw anyone. I'm sorry this happened. Is there anything I can do to help?"

"No thank you," Rhoda told her. "I should call the police. It had to be somebody who planned to break into our house but didn't want Buttons to bark. Larry says we don't have anything burglars would want, but you never know."

"You can't be too careful," Julianne said.

"I heard only last week about a woman two streets over who woke up in the middle of the night with burglars standing right there at the foot of her bed."

"How terrifying," Julianne said.

"I'm not going to worry about that right now," Rhoda said. "Buttons is recovering. Again, I'm sorry to bother you. I imagine you must be in a hurry to get to work."

"I am," Julianne said. "Are you sure that you and Buttons are okay?"

The dog barked in the background as if in response.

Julianne smiled. "She sounds like she's doing all right now."

"She is." Rhoda's voice was suddenly tearful. "She was so sick when she woke me. I was afraid she wouldn't even make it to the vet."

"She's fine," Larry called out. "From now on, we're going to keep her inside and stay with her when she has to go out."

Time was wasting, and they had to get going. David caught Julianne's eye and pointed to the clock.

"I'm sorry, but I have to go," Julianne said. "I've missed a couple of days at work, and I don't want to be late today. I also need to drop off some clothes at the dry cleaner's on the way. But I'll definitely keep my eyes open for anybody suspicious around the neighborhood."

"Thanks, dear," Rhoda said with a wistful sigh. "I'm glad you're feeling better. You be careful on the road."

"Thanks." Julianne disconnected.

"I guess our visitor last night didn't want Buttons to make any noise," David remarked.

"How could anyone poison such a sweet little dog?" Julianne asked. "She hardly ever barks anyway."

"She doesn't sound like a very good watchdog," he said. "She didn't make a sound when I arrived Monday night."

"Buttons stays in the house most of the time," Julianne said. "I don't know why she would have been out last night. They have a dog door, but she's always inside after dark. I feel awful for Rhoda. She doesn't get out much, and Buttons means the world to her."

"I'm glad Buttons and Rhoda are fine," David said. "I packed your things. Is there anything else we should take?" He spotted a phone charger on the nightstand and stuffed it into her suitcase. "Anything else?"

She scanned the bedroom, then shook her head. "We'd better go, if we're going to."

David picked up her suitcase and followed her into the garage. "Would you open the trunk?"

Julianne pressed the button on the key fob. "Is there enough room for you?"

"Yeah, I can fit." Inside the trunk were the bag of supplies and food that he'd already loaded and a battered box. He shoved them both along with her suitcase into the very back of the trunk, leaving just enough space for him. "Are you ready?"

She hesitated and glanced at the floor. "I hate that Rhoda is so upset."

"She said she was all right, and she has her son," he reminded her.

"I know."

"We've got to leave," David urged, taking her arm. "And we're not coming back."

"You're right," Julianne finally said. "I don't want to stay anyway."

David crawled into the trunk and curled up as best he could. He didn't like this part. The way he was bent was already making his side throb, and once she shut the lid, he would feel trapped and helpless. He forced a confident smile. "All right, get us out of here."

She hesitated, then slammed the trunk lid, plunging him into total darkness.

He took a deep breath and prayed they would make it out of town alive.

Julianne slid behind the wheel, pressed the button to open the garage door, and started the ignition. She sat there for a second, wondering what was going to happen next. Her life seemed so unreal. Ruthless criminals were after her. Her job and her home had been eerily arranged for her. Her dead husband was alive. How much more could she take?

"Please help me, God," she breathed. "Help me know what to do. Am I really supposed to drive away and leave my whole life behind? And then what?"

Julianne felt the car shift and knew David must be uncomfortable huddled inside the small trunk. She had to go. There was nothing more to do. Both their lives were in her hands now.

She backed out of the garage and down the driveway, then pulled into the street. Her dresses that were supposedly heading to the dry cleaner's hung in the window, her purse rested on the console next to her, and she was dressed for work. Nothing appeared out of the ordinary.

Larry was outside putting a couple of letters into his mailbox. As she drove past him, he smiled and waved like he always did when he happened to see her coming or going.

Julianne waved at Larry for the last time, wishing she had figured out a way to be nicer to him without giving him the wrong impression. It was too late now. She would never see her neighbor again.

As she went down the street, she was surprised to feel a twinge of regret. Not over Larry in particular, but she was going to miss Rhoda and her casseroles and her motherly worrying. And she would miss Buttons with her boundless energy and happiness.

But someone had tried to kill Buttons. Someone wanted to kill David. Possibly that same someone would kill her if he had the chance. There was no way around it. She had to flee.

Julianne pressed harder on the accelerator and headed toward her office, taking her usual route out of the neighborhood and toward downtown. As soon as she spotted an alley behind a church that she passed every day, she drove into it, stopped the car, and popped the trunk.

David scrambled out of the trunk and hopped into the front seat. "Go," he said, hunching down.

Before Julianne pulled onto the street, she studied David. He appeared pale and utterly spent.

"Anybody following us?" he asked.

She shook her head. "It's still early. There were a couple of cars when I left, but they turned off before this road. I haven't seen anyone get behind us and stay behind us."

"Good. First thing we need to do is ditch your phone somewhere. Permanently."

Julianne wanted to protest, but she knew he was right. Someone could trace her phone no matter where she was. They didn't have a whole lot of time now. She was expected at the office soon. Not long after that, Jim would be calling her to find out why she was late. She had to do something about her phone.

She reached over to her purse, grabbed her phone, and handed it to him. "What's the best way?"

"Can you pull into another alley?" David asked. "Somewhere we won't be seen?"

She nodded. Keeping to the side streets, she eventually parked behind a gas station.

He jumped out of the car and set the phone on the ground behind the front tire. "Back up."

Cringing, Julianne put the car into reverse, and she was rewarded with a crunching sound.

"Now pull forward and do it again," David said.

Resisting the urge to laugh, she backed over the phone and then pulled forward one more time. It was surreal.

"Good enough," David said, picking up the smashed phone from the concrete. He wiped off his fingerprints with his T-shirt and tossed the phone's shattered remains into a trash receptacle. "One more thing." He opened the door, moved her dresses into the trunk, and got into the front seat. "Let's go."

"What now?" she asked as they continued driving.

"Better get me a couple of changes of clothes and a razor and that kind of thing," David said. "And I need a burner phone. I have to call Mack and find out where we're going."

Julianne kept her eyes on the road. "There's a big-box store not far from here. It should have everything you need."

"It'll also have security cameras," he pointed out.

"Do you want to try somewhere else?" she asked.

"No, most stores will have security cameras anyway," David said. "You can buy me a basic phone. I don't like the idea of you going into the store without me, but I think it's better if we're not seen together yet. At least not right here in Springfield."

"What about clothes?"

"We'll stop at a thrift store," he answered.

They drove in silence until they arrived in the crowded parking lot of the big-box store.

"While you're in there, pick up a baseball cap," David said, handing her a few bills. "Black or navy. Something dark."

"Something dark," she repeated.

"We need to stop at an ATM when we get out of town too," he said.

"I don't have much in the bank," she told him.

"No, you can't withdraw any money from your accounts," David said sternly. "Don't use your credit cards. Don't do anything that can be traced back to you. Understand?"

She nodded, but her uneasiness grew. "What will we do about cash?"

"I have some on me, and I can get more at an ATM," he said. "I don't think they'll be able to trace me through this particular account."

"Anything else?" Julianne asked.

"Ask the clerk to activate the phone for you," David said. "You don't have to give them your ID or anything. In fact, why don't you leave your purse in the car? You don't need it, and that way they won't expect you to have anything."

"All right," she said.

"One more thing," he said. "Try not to give the impression that you're on the run."

Julianne couldn't quite smile at his teasing comment. She got out of the car, raised her head, straightened her shoulders, and strode into the store.

She picked up a baseball cap first because she passed it on the way to the electronics department located at the rear of the store. The cap was navy, and it didn't have any words or logos on it. Very anonymous.

The young clerk in the electronics department acted more bored than nosy. He activated the phone and didn't ask her any questions. He also rang up the baseball cap for her.

After accepting the bag and her change from the clerk, Julianne walked briskly back to the car, trying to appear casual. She handed David the bag and his remaining cash.

He smiled and put on the baseball cap. "Thanks. It's perfect." He unlocked the phone. "Now I can call Mack."

She backed out of the parking space and drove to the street.

"Is there a thrift store out this way?" David asked.

"I'm not sure," Julianne said, slowing down and scanning the area. "This isn't where I usually shop. You go ahead and make your call. I'll find something."

He dialed a number. A moment later, he abruptly hung up. "Voice mail."

"Why didn't you leave a message and tell him to call you?" she asked.

"I don't want a record of my call or risk anyone recognizing my voice," David said. "I'll try him again later."

Julianne drove for a few minutes, then parked in front of a thrift shop called Tammy and Terry's Treasures. It was next to a place that billed itself as a music store, but it seemed more like a pawnshop that had a few musical instruments in it.

"Is this store okay?" she asked.

"It's fine." He pulled the cap down lower. "Come on. I don't want you out here alone. This isn't the safest neighborhood."

David found a couple of pairs of jeans that were definitely used but not too worn. He also found a few T-shirts and polo shirts that were in very good shape.

"What about this?" Julianne asked, showing him a beat-up duffel bag that appeared to be from the military.

David grinned. "That's a good idea."

He paid cash for all of it, and they returned to the car.

"So where to next?" she asked.

"I still need razors and other necessities," he said. "How about stopping at a dollar store? They should have what I need. But first, let's make it as far out of town as possible."

Julianne started the car and headed east. "I'm not sure what's out here, but there should be a dollar store somewhere along the way."

They found a likely place not far from the highway. They were in and out of the store in a few minutes. Along with the necessities, David grabbed a bag of chocolate and winked at her. It was the kind they both liked.

Nothing was expensive, but she couldn't help wondering how much cash he had with him.

"I'm going to try Mack again," he said when they got into the car, "and you find us an out-of-the-way ATM."

This time when he called Mack, someone answered.

"Hey, Phil," David said heartily. "It's Tom Davis from the seminar."

Julianne could barely make out what the other man was saying.

"Tom Davis?" he repeated. "Oh, wait a minute. Are you talking about the seminar in Los Angeles?"

David's expression changed, but his voice didn't. "Yeah, man. How are you?"

"Great. And it's great to hear from you. What's up?"

"I was hoping you could hook me up with Whitman," David replied. "I know he was looking for guys to work for him."

"Nah, sorry. He's practically on the street these days. His company went belly-up last year. You'd probably have better luck trying something in New York."

David frowned. "That's too bad. I was hoping to locate some good opportunities and at least get my name out there, but I guess I'll keep up the search. Are you still in touch with Martindale?"

"Unfortunately, he's not doing well, and I haven't heard from him in months. You might try Eversleigh, but you'll have to move fast on that one. He's got a lot going on. Sorry, but that's all I've got. I wish I could help you, but I've been struggling myself. You know how it is."

"Yeah," David said. "Thanks for giving it to me straight. Maybe we can get together sometime. Have a burger or something."

"Sounds good. Give me a call when you're free, but don't wait around on Eversleigh. You might not get another chance. I'd better get going. Take care."

"Sure. Talk to you later." David ended the call, blowing out a breath as he slid the phone into his pocket.

Julianne parked near an ATM outside a small grocery store. She regarded the store's faded red-and-white sign. It looked like it had been there since the 1950s. *The Howdy-Do Mart*, it read in letters that resembled loops of rope. A cartoon cowboy slouched against the capital *T*.

"I don't think anybody will be expecting us to be here," David said with a tight smile. "Be right back."

After he got the cash, they moved on. He hadn't said anything about where they were going, so she got on the nearest highway and drove. He didn't object.

"What did Mack tell you?" Julianne finally asked. "I mean, I heard what he said, but I'm guessing that was some kind of code."

"He mentioned Los Angeles to tell me somebody was with him, so he couldn't talk," David explained. "If he'd said the seminar had been in New York, that would have meant he was alone and it was safe to have a conversation. 'Martindale' and 'Whitman' are different safe houses we use. But when he told me those guys had fallen on hard times, I knew they weren't safe anymore."

"What about 'Eversleigh'?" she asked.

"Between me and Mack, 'Eversleigh' means disappear," he answered. "Mack added that I should move soon because Eversleigh has a lot going on."

"So that means we need to disappear fast," Julianne concluded.

Her pulse kicked up a notch, and she pushed slightly harder on the accelerator, not taking her eyes off the road.

"There's a reason we use the name Eversleigh," David said quietly. "He was one of our agents who disappeared a couple of years ago. Even the bureau doesn't know what happened to him."

"That's terrible," Julianne remarked.

"We didn't set him up with a new identity," David said. "There's no evidence he was killed. We haven't heard anything about him on the street except from the guys he was collecting evidence on. They still want to get him, but from the information we have, they don't have a clue where he is either."

"I'm sorry," she said. "Did Mack tell you what you're supposed to do?"

"No, only that he's willing to see me if I can get to him."

"I think I've met him before," Julianne said as a memory suddenly clicked in her mind. "Is his first name Jeff?"

"Yeah, Jeff Macklin," David said, turning to face her. "When did you meet him?"

"When you started mentioning him, I thought his name sounded familiar," she said. "I realized that he might have been one of the people at your funeral who talked to me. Is he tall and blond?"

"Yes, that's Mack," he replied. "What did he want?"

"He told me that he worked with you at the IRS," Julianne said. "Then he gave me the box of your things from the office, including the notebook. Everything was in the box I have in the trunk now."

"Can you pull over?" he asked.

She raised her eyebrows. "Right this minute?"

"Whenever you get a chance," he said. "Don't make it seem suspicious. Pull off somewhere we won't be noticed."

It was getting hard to find places they wouldn't be noticed. Julianne checked the clock in the dashboard. It was well past time for her to be at work. She hadn't called in. What was left of her phone was in a trash receptacle many miles behind them. Jim couldn't call her to ask where she was. He must know by now that she had fled.

"They're already trying to find me, aren't they?" she asked.

"Probably." David glanced at the cars behind them. "I don't think we've been followed, but we don't have much of a head start, especially after stopping off at different places."

"Maybe they won't expect it," Julianne said. "They might assume we're hundreds of miles away on the highway somewhere. Even in another state or on our way to Canada."

"Where are we going anyway?" he asked.

"To the Spielmanns' cabin on Sangchris Lake," she replied. "Rhoda gave me the key and offered to let me use it whenever I felt like getting away."

"Then she'd expect you to go there," David said.

"No, I don't think so. I already told her that I don't have any vacation time accrued at work yet and that it would have to wait. Besides, there's no one for her to tell."

"Maybe not," he said. "But they'll be searching the house, and they'll most likely pay your neighbors a visit. These guys will intimidate them into giving you up. You'd better pull over here."

Julianne exited the highway and stopped the car behind an abandoned building. "Now what?"

"I can't help but wonder if Fulton is searching not only for us but for something specific," David said. "I want to know exactly what was in the box Mack gave you." He unbuckled his seat belt. "Pop the trunk for me, will you?"

She pulled the lever that unlatched the trunk. "I brought almost everything from the box into the house. The picture of me on the fridge, your coffee mug, and your notebook. It wasn't much."

He nodded. "I examined all that when I was there."

Julianne was a bit surprised. He hadn't mentioned it before.

They both went around to the back of the car. She watched David lift the trunk lid and search inside. Most of the contents in the cardboard box were items she kept in case of an emergency, such as a tire iron, a spare jacket, a compact umbrella, a portable radio, and that cheap little rug.

"Mack didn't bring you any of this?" he asked.

"Just the rug," she said, pushing her pile of dresses out of the way so she could pull out the rug. "It was in the box with the other stuff from your office."

David took the rug and unrolled it. "This was never in my office."

David flipped the rug over and examined the back of it. Then he ran his hands over it, twisting it and squeezing it. He'd never seen it before. Why had it been in the box with the rest of his belongings?

"Where did the rug come from?" Julianne asked. "I assumed it had been in your office because it was in the box."

"It must have gotten in with my stuff by mistake." He shook out the rug and twisted it again. "Maybe Fulton's men aren't searching for what was inside the box. They might be after the box itself."

David removed everything from the box and piled it into the trunk. He scrutinized the box itself, turning it over and pulling out the flaps in the bottom so he could see every bit of the cardboard.

It was just a box.

Julianne watched him, and he noticed the worry and mistrust in her eyes.

"I guess this box came from the office. It had copier paper in it." David pointed at the logo on one side of it. "That's the brand we use." He squinted, trying to see if there was something concealed in the product number or description printed below the logo. "I don't notice anything unusual, but we'd better hang on to it anyway. Mack can check into it later."

"But he's the one who gave it to me," Julianne reminded him. "Why would he pass it to me if he didn't want Fulton's men to find it?"

"I'm not sure," David admitted. "Since my alter ego was dead, maybe he believed that you weren't in any danger."

He replayed his conversation with Mack. "I've been struggling myself," his friend had said. What had Mack been trying to communicate? That he didn't have an available safe house for David to go to? Or had he also run into trouble with Fulton's men? David didn't make any other speculations, because he didn't want to worry Julianne with his bleak thoughts.

"Perhaps there's someone at the bureau he doesn't trust," she suggested.

He exhaled heavily. "That's possible. Mack might have thought that it would be safe with you because you don't have a clue what it is. Especially after all this time. Maybe he was waiting until he knew how it fit into Fulton's operation before he came for it."

"Do you think he knows someone's after it right now?" Julianne asked.

"If so, that would explain why he told us to get clear as fast as we could."

She stared at the flattened box. "So you can't trust the bureau to help us out, can you?"

David didn't want to respond, especially since she already knew the answer. "We need to get going again." He shut the trunk and put one arm around her shoulders. "Come on."

She stood perfectly still for a moment, and he hoped she might melt into his arms the way she used to do when she was troubled and needed comfort. Instead, she stepped away and got behind the wheel.

David couldn't blame her. He'd botched everything five months ago, and now he was making it even worse. But as horrible as their situation was, he was glad and relieved that she was beside him. She had no idea how much he'd missed her and how desperately he still loved her.

When he was at her house, he'd picked up the coffee mug that he had kept at the office and felt the solid weight of it in his hand. He'd remembered what the ampersand had meant to them.

David had also gazed at the picture of her on the door of her refrigerator. It had always been one of his favorites. He loved her wistful expression and beautiful smile that barely touched her lips. He liked trying to imagine what she'd been thinking about when he'd taken the picture, but he never wanted her to tell him. That would ruin the mystery.

David hadn't told Julianne any of that. He didn't have time to think about it. Not now. When they were out of this, when he finally got them somewhere safe, he would describe those long months without her, knowing she was grieving for him and then for her mother. Knowing how devastated she was to lose their house, all the artwork she had poured so much of her heart and soul into, and every trace of the life they'd had together. He vowed to make it up to her somehow.

He slid into the front seat beside her, and they got back on the highway.

"What are you thinking?" David asked, keeping his eyes on the mirror beside him. He saw no indication that anyone was following them.

"You really want to know?"

"Yes," he replied, bracing himself.

Julianne took a deep breath. "I'm thinking it was easier when I thought you were dead."

David managed not to wince. There was no anger in her tone, so she wasn't trying to be hurtful. She was being honest. Somehow it hurt him even more than if she'd been furious with him. "I'm sorry."

What else could he say? He was sure it was true. But what she thought of him right now didn't matter. Maybe they could work it out later. Maybe they never would. They had to stay alive first.

"Do you still think we should go to this cabin your neighbors have?" David asked.

She waited for a truck to pass them before changing lanes. "You talked to Mack. He wasn't very much help."

"I'll try him again in a little while. In the meantime, we should start heading his way. He's in Joliet." He grinned, trying to lighten the mood. "The town, not the prison."

Julianne didn't smile.

"I think we should go in that direction anyway," David said. "I have to talk to him. We need his help." He motioned to a road sign. "We can take the next exit and turn around."

She didn't say anything as she sailed past the exit.

"Tell me what you have in mind," he said.

"I told you that Rhoda has a cabin at the lake," Julianne replied. "It's southeast of Springfield. There's no reason anyone will know we're there."

David shook his head. "We have to get to Mack."

"Isn't there somebody else at the FBI you could go to?"

"There's no one else I completely trust," he answered. "Mack's the one I've been working with on this case. We wouldn't have gotten Mike Fulton without him."

"So his son will be after Mack too, right?"

"Yes, if Paul knew Mack existed. But I was the one they found out about. Mack's been way in the background. He was my sole contact at the bureau once I went undercover. It's crucial that I see him, so we need to go to Joliet."

"And then what?" she demanded. "When is this nightmare going to be over?"

"I don't know," David admitted. "Will you please try to trust me? This is my job and what I was trained to do. I can't tell you anything more until I find out what's going on. I can only promise you I'm going to do everything in my power to get us both somewhere safe. But you have to let me do my job."

Julianne stared straight ahead as if she hadn't heard a word he'd said. After a few moments, she signaled and moved into the right lane. She took the next exit and pulled a U-turn, heading back the way they'd come.

Toward Joliet.

They drove without saying much. David didn't know if Julianne was angry or preoccupied or afraid. Probably all of the above. It didn't feel like a good time to try to make small talk, but the silence was thick and taut, and the time passed slowly.

"Are you hungry?" he finally asked. "We haven't had anything since breakfast, and that was early this morning."

"Yeah," she said, giving him the tiniest smile. "I'm getting tired of driving too."

"You want me to take over?" David asked.

"Maybe after lunch," Julianne said. "How are you feeling?"

The wound was a dull ache in his side, but he could mostly ignore it. "I'm all right, but I could use a bite to eat. Something with meat."

"Can we go to a sit-down restaurant, or do we need to stop at a drive-through?"

"We can go inside if we find a restaurant that's off the highway," he answered. "When we stop, I'll try to call Mack again."

Julianne took the next exit. As he had requested, she drove off the highway and parked in front of an old gas station that had been renovated into a restaurant.

"You used to like this place," she said. "So did I."

"Yeah, it was good." David smiled, remembering how they had driven here when they were dating. "But we'd better not eat here. We don't need anybody recognizing your car."

"It's a gray Accord," Julianne said. "There must be millions of them."

"Still, it would be better to go to Mama's," he told her. "It's more out of the way and not as busy."

She didn't say anything else as she took side streets to a strip mall with a small restaurant on one end. It was located in a quiet old neighborhood, and two cars were parked out front.

"Let me try Mack first." David dialed the agent again.

It rang five times before a computer-generated voice answered. It repeated the number and announced it was currently unavailable.

David sighed and hung up.

They entered the restaurant. He stood for a moment inside the doorway, letting his eyes adjust to the dim light.

"Welcome," the hostess said. "Please follow me." She grabbed two menus and ushered them to a table in the middle of the room.

David motioned toward a vacant corner booth. "Can we sit there instead? We have some private things to talk about."

"Certainly." The hostess escorted them to the booth and handed them the menus. "Kevin will be with you soon."

A few moments later, a tall young man with dark hair bounded over to the table and beamed at them. "Hi, I'm Kevin. What can I get you to drink?"

"A cup of coffee, please," Julianne said. "Cream, no sugar."

"I'll have the same," David said.

"Two coffees," Kevin said. "You take your time with the menu.

Our special today is lasagna with salad and garlic bread, and I definitely recommend it."

"You're in an awfully chipper mood for somebody who has to work for a living," David joked.

"I always look on the bright side." Kevin grinned. "Besides, I have a big reason to be happy."

"Oh yeah?" David asked.

"I usually work nights," Kevin said. "We have a lot more business then, and I get better tips. But today I traded shifts with a coworker because my girlfriend and I are going to have dinner and then see a play." He beamed. "After that, I'm going to ask her to marry me."

David couldn't help but smile too. "Congratulations." He shook Kevin's hand. "I've made some pretty poor decisions in my time, but marrying my wife sure wasn't one of them. When it's the right one, it's the right one, and nobody else will do."

"Karen's definitely the right one," Kevin assured him.

"How long have you two known each other?" Julianne asked.

"We met in second grade," Kevin said. "We won't get out of college until next spring, and I figure that will be soon enough to actually tie the knot."

Julianne glanced at David, then addressed Kevin. "I hope you and Karen have a wonderful life together."

David and Julianne had met in grade school too. Their classes had forced them together, but he recalled they hadn't hit it off. During middle school, something changed between them. A few of the other boys noticed Julianne, and David realized he didn't like it. He managed to run into her around the neighborhood several times, and they started hanging out together. When they entered high school, they began going on actual dates, something that continued when they went to college. He'd never wanted to be with anyone else.

"Do you want some advice from an old married man?" David asked him.

"Sure," Kevin said.

"Always tell her the truth."

Kevin sobered, nodding.

"If you can't tell her the truth, then you shouldn't get married," David advised.

"Thanks," Kevin said. "I'll remember that."

"Do you think he'll always tell her the truth?" Julianne asked David after Kevin left to get their drinks.

"I hope so," he said. "It'll save them both a lot of grief."

Kevin returned with their cups of coffee, and they both ordered the lasagna special.

While they waited, Julianne reflected on David's conversation with their waiter. She wished David had always told her the truth. Maybe then they wouldn't be stuck in this disturbing predicament.

Soon Kevin delivered their meals and refilled their coffee cups.

As they ate, Julianne tried to keep up her end of the conversation, but it was hard not to jump every time the front door opened and more people entered the restaurant. She knew David had his gun in the pocket of his jacket, but that knowledge didn't make her feel much more secure, especially when she had to walk down the long hallway at the rear of the restaurant to go to the ladies' room.

"I tried to call again while you were gone," David said quietly when she returned to the table. "Still no answer."

Julianne had a sinking feeling in the pit of her stomach. "What now?"

"We keep driving. And keep trying."

David paid the check and left Kevin a very generous tip. *Best wishes on your life together*, he wrote on the back of the bill. *God bless you both*.

Julianne smiled. David was so sweet, but he could also be frustrating sometimes. She needed to be sure of what was ahead, even if it was terrifying and dangerous. At least it would put an end to this endless waiting, always wondering when someone was going to kick down the door and shoot them.

It sounded ridiculously melodramatic in light of the fact that she hadn't actually seen anything the least bit out of the ordinary. But she couldn't take any of this lightly. Either David was finally telling her the truth, or this was all some kind of elaborate scheme for him to get her back after abandoning her five months ago.

Julianne didn't know if she'd ever feel safe again. She didn't know if she'd ever *be* safe again.

When they walked to the car, he opened the passenger door for her and then got behind the wheel.

David tried once more to reach Mack. "Still no answer," he told her. "I guess we keep heading to Joliet."

Their destination should have been about another two and a half hours away, but he decided they should backtrack, just in case. He drove into an alley, got out of the car so he could grind the burner phone into pieces under his heel, and tossed the remnants into the trash can behind a fast-food restaurant. After that, he drove north until they arrived in Bloomington.

"We need to get two more burner phones," he said as he parked in the lot of a big-box store. "Maybe Mack isn't answering calls from that first number because he doesn't want anybody to trace us through him. Plus, if we keep changing numbers, it'll be harder for anybody to trace us."

She hoped he was right.

Julianne didn't consider not going in with him. She felt too vulnerable sitting out in the car alone. Unarmed. She knew he would have left the gun with her if she'd asked him to, but he was the one who knew how to use it. In an emergency situation, the person with the gun needed to be experienced enough to act without hesitating. She didn't have that experience, and now wasn't the time to try to get it.

When they returned to the car, David called Mack, but he didn't answer.

David pulled onto the highway and drove north toward Joliet. They were about halfway there when traffic came to an abrupt standstill.

Julianne tried to see what was causing the problem ahead of them, but an enormous moving van was stopped in front of the car, and she couldn't see anything else. "Can you tell anything from your side?"

David shook his head, drumming his fingers on the steering wheel.

They sat for several minutes, not moving an inch. Then David exited the car, walked around it, and peered behind them.

Finally, David jumped back into the car. "I don't see a thing. It must be an accident farther up the road." He scanned the area again. "At this point, the only way we're moving is on foot."

"We're trapped here," she said, starting to panic. "Do you think Fulton's people shut the road down to capture us?"

"It's incredibly unlikely that even they could shut down a whole interstate to get us." He grinned. "Plus, they would somehow have to know that we'd be here at this exact moment."

His smile helped her to calm down. "So now what?"

"We wait," David said. "We'll relax and catch up. I never told you—"

He was interrupted by someone pounding on the driver's side door.

Julianne whirled around, sure her heart would beat right out of her chest.

"Can I help you?" David asked, slowly rolling down the window.

Julianne noticed that his other hand rested on the gun in his jacket pocket.

A middle-aged man stood at the door. "Sorry. I didn't mean to startle you." He smiled at them.

Julianne thought the man appeared harmless in his rumpled suit with a tie hanging loose from his collar. She reminded herself that she'd thought Jim was nice, but he'd turned out to be working for Fulton. She remained on edge, hoping this man wasn't one of them too.

"I saw you walking around," the man continued, "and I was wondering if you found out what's going on."

"No, I don't know anything," David said. "I'm assuming it was an accident, so we might be stuck here for a long time."

"It sure seems like it," the man said. Then he grinned. "Guess I'll go and start on the great American novel I always said I was going to write."

David chuckled. "Good luck."

The man laughed and walked away.

Julianne flipped down the mirror on her sun visor and watched the man climb into a green hatchback.

"I should be kicked for not being more careful," David said. "If he saw me, who else did?"

"Do you think we should be worried about him?" she asked, facing him.

"It's not always easy to say, but I'd guess not," he replied. "He didn't appear to have a weapon. Again, it would be hard for them to have known ahead of time where we were so they could stop us here and send someone to verify that it was us."

"Unless he's been following us all along," Julianne reasoned.

David shook his head. "Not in that car anyway."

"That you're aware of," she said.

The moving van in front of them rolled forward about three feet, and David did the same.

"You've got to trust me," he said. "Or at least try."

It wasn't a plea. It wasn't a reproof. It was a statement.

"I'm doing the best I can for us," David added. "That's what I've always tried to do."

Julianne nodded. She knew it was true. In fact, it was one of the things she loved most about him. When he'd left, she'd missed knowing that no matter what happened, there was someone there for her, someone who would live and die for her sake. As David had always done.

The van ahead of them inched forward, and they followed until they finally reached the next exit. Fortunately, they were already in the right lane. After what seemed like an eternity of stopping and going, they managed to escape the highway.

Of course, the access road and the roads that connected to it were flooded with other cars trying to get away from the snarl. David drove east for a while before steering north again.

"Maybe it's a blessing in disguise," he commented. "We'll take the back way. At this point, how could anybody predict which way we're going?"

A terrifying thought popped into her head, and she gasped. "Oh no!"

"What?" David asked, glancing at her.

"Perhaps they don't need to follow us or figure out which way we're going," Julianne said. "What if they put something on my car to track me? If they've set me up all along, they could have done it anytime."

"Don't worry," he said. "I checked the car out before we left, and I didn't notice anything. Unless it's an elaborate tracking device, which I don't think they'd feel was necessary for you, I believe we're okay."

"What do you mean?" she asked. "Why wouldn't they use something like that for me?"

"If they planted anything, it probably would have been right after they got you settled into the house and the job," David answered. "There would be no reason for you to suspect anyone was keeping tabs on you, so they would do something simple that most people wouldn't think to look for."

"That makes sense," Julianne said.

"Besides, your car's been in the garage ever since I showed up," he added. "If they were going to plant something on you because they assumed we'd be taking off once I got there, they wouldn't have had an opportunity to do it."

"Do you think they sent someone to try last night when Buttons was poisoned?" she asked.

"We would have heard it if someone attempted to open the garage door," David said. "I'd guess it was someone who was trying to find out whether or not I was anywhere around."

Julianne shivered as she pictured someone prowling around her house and yard, watching them.

He shrugged. "It doesn't matter now. Once I talk to Mack, he'll get us a different car and new IDs, and then we can move on. Maybe it won't even have to be for very long."

"Where do you think we'll go?" she asked.

"I don't know," he admitted. "We have to take it one step at a time for now, all right?"

Julianne nodded. She didn't have any other choice.

When they made it to Joliet, David tried one last time to reach Mack, but he had no luck. David's expression was strained as he disconnected.

Julianne was worried about him. She knew he was exhausted and his wound needed to be cleaned and bandaged. "Are you okay? Maybe we should take a break so you can rest."

For a moment, she thought he'd refuse and want to push on.

"Yeah, let's stop at a motel," he agreed, gripping the steering wheel.

"Can we rent a room without identification?" she asked.

"We'll find a place that will take cash." David drove down a seedy street, then parked in an alley near The Driftwood Court Motel.

He gave her a sardonic grin. "I'm not sure where the driftwood part came from, since I doubt this place has been near water since God separated the sea from the land, but here we are."

Julianne regarded the shabby motel with a long line of doors and windows under a sagging overhang. At the end was a slightly larger section that was probably the lobby and reception area. "It reminds me of the Bates Motel."

David snickered. "If the desk clerk's name is Norman, we'll go somewhere else." He removed a few bills from his wallet and handed them to her. "Go in. Pay for three nights."

"Three?" she repeated. "Please don't tell me we're staying here that long."

"No, but it won't hurt for them to think you'll be around for a few days." He exited the car. "I'll wait outside until you get a room and then join you."

Julianne got behind the wheel. "Don't be long."

He walked over to a telephone pole and leaned against it. "I'll be right here."

She drove to the front of the motel, parked under the metal awning, and hurried through the front door.

The young woman behind the desk appeared to be in her late twenties. Her waist-length hair cascaded down her shoulders from a knot at the top of her head. She was reading *David Copperfield*, and a yellow parakeet slept on her shoulder.

Julianne stood awkwardly for a moment. She noticed the clerk's name tag read *Dot*.

"Just the one?" Dot asked, not glancing up from her book.

"Yes."

Dot slid an index card between the pages of her book and shoved it aside. "Got a favorite number?"

Julianne smiled slightly, puzzled.

"Except it can't be three," Dot said, "because three's taken."

"How about fifteen?" Julianne asked. She'd noticed that room was at the end of the long row, and it was located near a big white oak that shaded the parking lot. Maybe the car would be less noticeable parked under the tree, especially when night fell.

"Fifteen will do." Dot grabbed a key with a green plastic tag that had a black number *15* emblazoned on it and pushed it across the counter. "No pets. No smoking. No firearms. No more than eight people in the room. Checkout's at eleven in the morning. After that, you have to pay for another day."

"I was hoping to stay for three nights," Julianne said. "If you're not completely booked already."

Dot snorted. "We're not booked." She gave the total for three nights. "No checks."

"Can I pay with cash?" Julianne asked. "Or is that a problem?"

"Cash is fine," Dot said matter-of-factly.

Julianne handed her the money.

Dot took it and then returned to her book. The parakeet never woke up.

Julianne left the office and got into the car. She pulled around to the door that had a black plastic *15* screwed onto it, parked under the tree, and popped the trunk to retrieve the few things they had brought along with them, including the bag of food. She could definitely use a bite of chocolate right now.

She considered bringing in the cardboard box, but she decided to let David get it if he thought it was important to keep with them. Maybe he would bring the little rug inside too. It was about as useless as the box, but it had been in the box from David's office.

After slamming the trunk shut, Julianne carried the bags and her suitcase to the door. She scanned the area and spotted David. He stood partially concealed behind the trunk of the oak, waiting for her.

He walked over to her, then took the key and unlocked the door. "Stay here." With his gun drawn, he entered the room.

A few moments later, David came back to the door and nodded.

Julianne went inside and locked the door behind her.

David took the bags and suitcase from her and set them down on the floor by the bed.

She studied the tiny room. She had expected to be fighting off cockroaches with one hand and enormous rats with the other, but despite being in desperate need of paint and general maintenance, the room was actually quite clean. Even the sheets smelled fresh. Her fear of bedbugs receded.

Julianne tossed her purse onto one of the plastic chairs and sat down on the bed. It was surprisingly comfortable. "You should rest."

David stretched out on the bed and set the gun within reach. He groaned. "I don't think I could have remained vertical for another ten minutes."

"Are you all right?" Julianne put her hand on his forehead. He felt warmer than before. "You'd better take some ibuprofen." She poured him a glass of water from the tap and gave him the bottle of medicine.

David swallowed the pills and drank the water, then sank back onto the bed and closed his eyes. "Wake me up in a couple of hours." He didn't wait for her answer before falling fast asleep.

Trying to be as quiet as possible, Julianne packed David's new things into the duffel bag from the thrift shop and sorted through everything else they'd brought. She compacted it as much as possible, tossing the trash from the new items into one of the shopping bags to be thrown away somewhere else.

It didn't take long, and then there was nothing else for her to do. She turned on the bolted-down TV but kept the volume low to avoid disturbing David.

As Julianne watched an old sitcom, she snacked on chocolate and couldn't help but wonder what they would do next. She was still planning to go to the cabin because she believed that Fulton's men wouldn't be able to find them there, but she was losing confidence in the plan. David didn't seem to like the idea, and he was the one with experience in these kinds of situations. Perhaps Mack would have a better alternative for them. Whatever they did, there was no way she was staying in this motel for more than one night.

It was late before David stirred again.

"What time is it?" he asked.

She switched off the television and went to him. "Are you feeling better?"

"Much." He glanced at the gun next to him and sat up. "You shouldn't have let me sleep so long."

"You obviously needed the rest," Julianne said. She felt his forehead again, but he seemed a little cooler. "Are you sure you don't need a doctor?"

"No, I'm all right."

"Good. I—" She yawned and belatedly covered her mouth. "Sorry. It seems I'm more tired than I thought."

"Go ahead and sleep," he said. "I'll keep watch now. Have you seen or heard anything I should know about?"

"Nothing. I don't know how this motel stays open if they don't have more business than this."

"It'll pick up," David said. "You wouldn't want to know what happens in a place like this during the weekend."

Julianne cringed.

He got up and helped himself to some of the chocolate she'd been eating. "Go on," he said, nodding toward the bed. "You need your sleep. We'll get started again in the morning."

"You're not planning to stay up all night, are you?" she asked.

David shrugged. "I'm sure I'll doze off."

"Why don't you take a shower?" she asked. "Actually, why don't we take off your bandage and see how that wound is doing?"

After giving her a warning look, David hurried over to the television and turned it on. He flipped channels and stopped on a movie about

World War II. Then he adjusted the sound, so it would drown out their conversation.

"How does it feel?" she asked him.

He dutifully pulled up his shirt for her to inspect the wound.

Julianne examined him. His side remained red and swollen, but it wasn't as warm to the touch. It didn't feel like he had much of a fever, but she took his temperature anyway. It was just a little over a hundred.

"Not bad," she admitted. "If you're going to stay up, you should take a shower and change into your new clothes. Then we can rinse these out and let them dry overnight."

David glanced at the door. "Are you sure you're good with that?"

"I'm sure," she said.

"Do you want to hang on to this?" he asked, offering her the gun.

"We'd both be safer if you kept it," Julianne said. "But I was wondering if you wanted to get the box and rug out of the trunk and bring them in here."

"I don't see anything the least bit interesting about either one of them," David said as he set the gun on the nightstand. "But I'll get them just in case. I might check them out again to see if I notice something I didn't before."

She handed him the car keys and stood at the window, peeking around the edge of the curtain while he went out, retrieved the flattened box and the little rug, and walked back inside. Once more, she locked the door.

After briefly studying the two items, he put them down on the chair. "If you can, don't go to sleep until I get out of the shower. Let me know if you see or hear anything out of the ordinary, all right?"

Julianne nodded.

David grabbed the gun and his new clothes from the duffel bag.

As he headed to the bathroom, he peered out the window again. "You'd better keep watch. If you see anybody at all, come and get me."

She joined him at the window, but there was no one in sight. "I will."

"I'll be right out." He strode to the bathroom and shut the door.

Julianne scanned the room. Did she actually expect him to stay awake all night? Apart from the two plastic chairs, the narrow chest of drawers with the TV bolted on top of it, and the rickety nightstand, the bed was the only furniture in the room. There wasn't even enough floor space for him to stretch out on.

The sound of running water stopped. David would be out in a minute.

Julianne removed her pajamas and bag of toiletries from her suitcase. She might as well get clean and comfortable too. When she glanced at the TV, the soldiers in the movie were marching through a miserable swamp on a Pacific island. Just watching them made her long for soap and hot water.

She peeked around the curtain. Except for the car parked in front of the room three doors down and the one near the office that was most likely Dot's, the parking lot was empty. Everything was quiet.

"All yours," David said when he opened the bathroom door. "Everything okay?"

"Yeah, I haven't seen anything."

"Good." He sat down in one of the plastic chairs with the gun in his lap and started drying his hair with a towel.

Julianne remembered how his hair always curled when it was wet and how he would try to comb it smooth. He usually kept it too short to curl very much, but now it was long enough for a curl to fall over his forehead.

"Feeling better?" she asked.

"I am. Thanks. Do you have those bandages?"

She had packed the medical supplies in a separate small bag, and she took them out of her suitcase. "Any more bleeding?"

"No," David said. "I washed it, but I was careful. If you'll put some antibiotic ointment on it and wrap it, I think that's all it needs."

When Julianne examined the wound, she realized he was right. It was clean and healing. It didn't even feel warm anymore. She spread the antibiotic ointment on the area and carefully covered it with a square adhesive bandage.

"Thank you," he said, pulling his T-shirt down.

She tried to ignore the way David smelled like fresh soap. "You should have gone to the hospital. You're going to have a scar."

"I was going to have a scar anyway." He grinned. "As long as that scar's on a live body, I'm good."

She shook her head and picked up her pajamas and bag of toiletries. "I'll be out in a minute."

"We're going to get through this," David said firmly.

Julianne didn't respond. She went into the bathroom and closed the door behind her. For a long moment, she leaned against the wall, clutching her pajamas and her bag to her chest. She wanted to believe him. She wanted desperately to believe him.

She just didn't know if she could.

David stared at the television, watching the soldiers fight their way through the jungle, but he didn't really see them. He thought instead of Julianne, of all these months without her and what she had been through without him. Because of him.

He'd found out about her mother's death not long after it happened. She had been there for him after his own mother passed away when he was in his teens. When he and Julianne had gotten engaged, her mother had asked him if he wanted to call her Mom.

"Being called Mrs. Price makes me feel so old," she had said.

David had rushed over and hugged her, overjoyed that she felt the same way he did about their relationship. He was thrilled that his future mother-in-law would be someone he loved and was comfortable with. Two years later, when his father died, he was glad he had a mother to comfort him, grieve with him, and make him feel like he still had a family. Now she was gone, and Julianne had had to deal with her death completely alone.

As David continued staring at the screen, he considered calling Mack. But he quickly rejected the idea, then opened the bag of chocolates and popped a piece into his mouth. He focused on their next steps. They needed to get help and go somewhere safe. He had to figure out what Fulton and his people wanted and stop them. After that, David and Julianne could decide what to do about their relationship.

If there was any relationship left.

Julianne walked out of the bathroom, and David glanced up at her and smiled. Her blonde hair was piled on top of her head, and she wore flannel pajamas with bunnies on them.

"Kind of warm for flannel, isn't it?" he teased.

She shrugged. "I got them right after the fire. They made me smile when not much else did. I didn't want to leave them behind."

"That's understandable," David said. "It had to be a shock to lose everything all of a sudden."

"Yeah," she said softly. "It must have been the same for you when you left with nothing but the clothes you were wearing. It's hard."

"It is," David admitted. "But it's sort of liberating too. Instead of having things just because you've always had them, you can start over and get what you really need. What you really want."

"I hadn't thought about it like that, but I suppose it's true," Julianne said. "I guess that's why my house in Springfield didn't have much in it besides furniture."

"Are you still tired?" he asked.

"A little. But I'm not sleepy yet." She sat on the bed, facing his chair, and tucked her legs under herself. "Are you?"

"Yeah, but I'm not ready to go to sleep. I need to make sure we're not being watched."

Her body tensed. "Do you think we are?"

"I haven't seen any sign of it, but we can't take anything for granted," David said. "Since we're going to be here until morning at least, I was hoping we could talk." He took a steadying breath. "Tell me what I missed when I was gone. Do you still paint?"

"I haven't picked up a brush since you left," Julianne replied. "Mom encouraged me to start again. I even signed up for a class, hoping it would force me to paint on a regular basis. Then Mom got worse, and I never had a chance to go."

"That's a shame. You always enjoyed painting, and you have a real gift for it." He leaned forward in his chair. "Will you tell me about Mom?"

Her mouth tightened. David knew that look. She was trying not to cry.

"I'm sorry," he said, reaching over to cover her hand with his. "I realize it still hurts. It still hurts me too."

Her eyes filled with tears, but they didn't fall. "She loved you so much. When we thought you were dead, it was difficult for both of us. I hadn't seen her that upset since Dad died. She told me that you were her son as much as if she'd given birth to you and raised you, and she meant it."

"I know." David felt fresh guilt squeeze his heart. "Please tell me the truth. Do you think that she got worse because she believed I was dead?"

Julianne lowered her head.

"I was afraid of that." His voice was low and ragged, and it was a struggle to say it. He stared up at the ceiling and swallowed hard. "I'm sorry. I truly am. The last time you and I talked to her doctor, he said her condition was stable, and I was hoping that she would improve. I didn't want her to think I was dead, but . . ." He trailed off, not wanting to embarrass himself by breaking down in front of her.

She didn't say anything.

David removed his hand from hers.

Julianne caught his hand and held it. "No," she said softly, her voice almost lost in the sounds of the battle coming from the TV. "I don't think that was why she got worse. You know that Mom was a fighter."

He saw a small, trembling smile on her lips. The tears were still brimming in her eyes.

"She loved and missed you, but she didn't want to die," Julianne assured him. "She wanted to recover. She swore she was going to get better, because she didn't want me to be left alone. The night before the doctor planned to send her home, she had a stroke." She closed her eyes for a moment. "And then she was gone."

They were both still grieving. David wanted so much to comfort Julianne and be comforted by her, but he also knew that she was likely to misinterpret even a comforting touch. As much as he longed to take her into his arms and hold her close, he didn't dare. He didn't want her to have even the slightest reason to think he was trying to take advantage of her when she was frightened and vulnerable. He hoped she still loved him, and maybe she did. But until he proved that she could trust him again, it didn't matter.

David settled for squeezing her hand. "I hope Dannie was with you."

There was a touch of wryness in her smile. "She flew in the day of the funeral. She had a friend with her, and they left as soon as the service was over. Dannie said she was sorry, but they had to catch a flight because they were going on a cruise. They'd planned it months earlier, and it was nonrefundable."

Dannie's selfish actions didn't surprise David. It was his own absence during such a difficult time that really angered him. He hadn't been there for Mom, and he hadn't been there for Julianne.

Now David would never have that precious time to say goodbye, to let Mom know, however inadequately, what she'd meant to him. Julianne was here now, but how long would she stick around? If they survived this ordeal, would she stay with him? Or would she decide that too much had happened for them to be together again?

He shook his head. "I'm sorry that Dannie barely made time for Mom's funeral. It must have hurt."

"Yes and no," Julianne said. "It's not like Dannie spent much time talking to Mom since she moved to Seattle. Or even before, to be honest. But that's the way Dannie is. I didn't expect anything different from her." She frowned. "Before she left, she asked me what she needed to do to claim her part of the life insurance and when we could get started on the probate."

He reached for her other hand. "I'm sorry."

"Mom knew it would be that way," Julianne said. "That's why she made me her executor. She didn't have that much for us to inherit anyway, just what she had in the bank and her personal effects. She got rid of almost everything else before she went into the nursing facility. We decided that she'd move in with me when she got better. But that never happened."

David knew that grief took time. In the past, he'd tried to ignore it, but he'd simply had to deal with it later. It had been like that when his dad died. It was like that now with Julianne's mom. He hoped his wife would allow him to walk through this valley with her.

He squeezed her hands one more time before letting them go. "You must be exhausted from standing guard all day. Why don't you get some sleep? I'll keep watch."

"What if you can't get ahold of Mack?" she asked.

"We'll have to figure out something else," he answered.

"I know you already told me that you don't want to talk to anyone but Mack," Julianne said. "Will you reconsider? There must be someone else at the FBI who can help us."

He shook his head. "If Paul sent somebody after you because Mack gave you something from my office, then how would anybody be aware of it unless there was a leak in the bureau?"

"Are you sure it's not Mack?" she asked, her eyes hard.

"It's definitely not Mack," David said. "He's a good friend. Not to mention he was the one who got me out of that mess with Fulton in the first place."

Julianne snorted. "If you ask me, he didn't do such a great job since we're both in trouble now."

"Fulton knows that I'm still alive because I had to kill one of his guys," David said. "But I could have stayed gone. I would have been completely in the clear if I hadn't come back for you. If Mack's working for Fulton, why would he give you whatever it is they're searching for?"

"I don't know," she admitted.

"If Mack was the only one at the bureau who knew about it, then he could have simply kept it and given it to Fulton," he argued. "Fulton would have probably given him a bonus. Why involve you at all? Besides, like I said, I know Mack, and I trust him. I won't talk to anyone else."

"You should do what you think is best," Julianne responded, but she didn't sound convinced.

"I wouldn't have put you through any of this if it wasn't absolutely necessary," David said. "Whatever else happens, I need you to believe that."

She took a deep breath and then sighed. "What am I supposed to believe? I see you standing there, and I thank God that you're not dead. And the next minute, I realize that my whole life has been blown to smithereens because of you."

"But you still have a life." He took her hand once more. "At this point, that's all that matters."

"I guess you're right." Julianne pulled away and got into bed. She curled up on her side the way he remembered she always had, with the pillow bunched up under her head.

David wished this nightmare were over so that he could take his wife into his arms and hold her close. He desperately wanted to stop looking over his shoulder. To stop reaching for his gun at every sound. To stop wondering if the next moment would be his last.

He went to the TV and switched it off.

"Thank you," she said, watching him.

David shrugged. "You would have never gotten to sleep with World War II going on."

"No," she said softly. "I meant thank you for keeping me safe."

"I promised you that from the very beginning, didn't I?" He picked up the gun and sat down with it on his lap. "I'll never break that promise."

She murmured something he didn't catch and closed her eyes.

David knew Julianne was worried and scared, but somehow she went straight to sleep. She had the covers in both hands and her hands tucked under her chin, and her body was curled up as if she were in a safe little nest. She trusted him that much at least. Or maybe she was simply exhausted.

He switched off the light and moved his chair to the window, where he had a clear view of the car and the parking lot. It was going to be a long night, but he would keep his promise and make sure she remained safe.

No matter what.

"David."

The whisper jolted David out of a near sleep, and he instinctively felt for the gun in his lap. Not making a sound, he crept to the side of the bed next to Julianne. "What's wrong?"

"Do you see anything?" she asked.

"No," he answered. "Only two cars drove by in the past three hours."

"At least when you were awake," Julianne said. Her tone was light, almost teasing.

"I didn't actually fall asleep." David smiled, even though it was dark and he was sure she couldn't see it. "Not quite anyway."

"Why don't you sleep for a couple of hours?" she suggested. "I can keep watch."

"I'm fine," he said. "You need to get a full night's rest."

"You're still getting over being shot," she argued. "Not to mention you're the one who knows how to use the gun if we need it. There's no reason for you to be deprived of sleep when I can stay alert."

David huffed, but he couldn't argue with her.

"Come on," she said. "It'll be fine. If I see anybody in the parking lot, I promise I'll wake you up."

"You're being reasonable, and that ruins my attempt at being heroic," he joked.

Julianne laughed.

It was a soft, sleepy laugh, and it reminded him of all the times they had laughed and talked in the middle of the night. He wanted her to laugh—truly laugh—much more often than she had been.

"Okay, I'll sleep for a couple of hours," David relented. "Be sure to wake me up if you see anybody in the parking lot, any cars slowing down when they pass by, and especially if somebody enters the lobby. Deal?"

"Deal."

He heard the rustle of the sheets as she got out of bed, and he could barely distinguish her dark silhouette against the slightly lighter curtains as she sat down in the other chair.

David took the gun and crawled into the warmth of the bed, realizing that he'd been sitting a little bit sideways to keep from putting pressure on the bullet wound. He set the gun within easy reach and situated himself so he could relax from head to toe. It took a couple of minutes for the throbbing in his side to dull.

After that, he didn't remember anything.

David opened his eyes. The curtains were still closed, so it wasn't actually light in the room, but he could tell that it was lighter. How long had he been asleep?

He grabbed the gun that was resting next to him on the bed, leaned up on one elbow, and checked the alarm clock on the nightstand. It was nearly seven. Why had Julianne let him sleep so late?

David scanned the room to find her and then shook his head. She was curled up on her side, sound asleep. Clutching the pistol, he crept to the window and pulled the curtain aside. The sun was up, but the street was completely quiet. There was a car parked in front of the room three doors down and another one by the motel office. Like last night. That was all.

Gun still in hand, David went into the bathroom. He washed his face and brushed his teeth with the spare toothbrush he'd brought from Julianne's house. She was awake when he walked into the room, a patch of red on each cheek and her green eyes wide.

"Good morning," he said.

Julianne pushed one hand through her tousled hair. "I'm sorry. I didn't mean to fall asleep. I only shut my eyes for a minute. It was already light when I went to bed."

"It's fine. I fell asleep too." David grinned. "Nearly." He grabbed an apple from their supply of food. "Want one?"

"Yeah," she said. "For a start."

He tossed it to her, then took another apple and sat down on the bed to eat it. "You don't need to get up yet. I have to call Mack before we go."

"You don't think we should get out of here right away?" Julianne asked.

He studied her for a moment before walking over to the window. There was some traffic since it was Friday morning, a workday. There would be more and more traffic through here, even on this quiet little side street.

"I'll tell you what," David said, turning back to her. "If you feel like it, go ahead and get dressed. While you're getting ready, I'll try one more time to call Mack. We're going whether I talk to him or not. By then, there should be enough traffic on the road so we don't stick out. What do you think?"

"That sounds good," she said. "I don't want to stay here too much longer."

He pulled out one of the burner phones, then sat down on the bed and leaned against the headboard. "I promise we'll leave soon."

Without another word, Julianne collected her clothes and bag of toiletries and strode into the bathroom.

When she was gone, David dialed Mack's number.

"Yeah?" someone asked. It sounded as if whoever it was had been asleep.

David thought it was Mack, but he wasn't completely sure. "Phil?"

"Is this Tom Davis?"

"Yes," David said. He still wasn't certain if he was talking to Mack. "Is this Phil?"

"No, it's Mack."

David breathed a sigh of relief. "I'm so glad it's you. Did I wake you up? You didn't sound like yourself."

"I finally went to bed after being up for nearly forty hours straight." Mack cleared his throat and groaned. "Hang on while I put on some coffee."

"I'm sorry for waking you," David said. "Have you heard from Eversleigh lately?"

"No, I think he's in New York somewhere."

That meant Mack was alone and it was safe to talk. But David felt a little uneasy, so he asked another question to make sure everything was really okay. "How's Kathy?"

Mack laughed.

David could clearly picture him with his sun-bleached hair sticking up in messy spikes, his chin dark with unshaved stubble, and his hazel eyes bleary but glinting with humor.

"It's all right," Mack said. "Kathy had twins."

"Well, that's great news," David said, relieved to hear the all clear.

"Don't tell me where you are," Mack said. "But you need to get someplace safe for a while."

David's heart skipped a beat. "What have you heard?"

"Fulton knows you're not dead."

"I realize that," David said. "That was why he sent Farrar after Julianne. I had to get rid of him."

"Yeah, I know," Mack said. "One of his men spotted you on your way out of the building after you did it."

"Who?" David asked.

"Stover," Mack answered. "You remember that his brother was one of the guys killed at the wedding. He's not likely to forget you."

"Probably not."

"What about Julianne?" Mack asked. "Fulton's not going to give up on the first try."

"She's with me," David said.

"That's a relief." Mack was silent for a moment. "How did you get in and out of her house?"

"I walked through the woods to get to her place," David said. "It helped that there was a storm that night. But I wouldn't want to do it again. Not with a bullet wound."

"Are you okay?" Mack asked.

"I am now." David heard a beeping and assumed it was his friend's coffee maker.

"Ah, finally," Mack said. "Just a second while I pour a cup." A few moments later, he said, "Much better. So, did anyone see you making a break for it with Julianne?"

"No one saw us," David said. "And I'm sure we weren't followed. It's likely somebody was watching the house, but as far as he would have seen, Julianne was home sick for a couple of days, and then she drove to work. The earliest they could have wondered what was up was when she didn't show up at the office or call in sick yesterday. But that was after we'd already left and had gotten a head start."

"That's good news," Mack said, but he didn't sound very convinced.

"We've changed directions enough since we left that I don't think Fulton's guys have a clue where to even start searching," David continued. "But we've got to find somewhere safe. We can't keep running like this. We need a different car, new IDs, the works."

"I already told you that the Whitman and Martindale places aren't safe anymore," Mack said. "I'm doing what I can to get you somewhere, but you have to lie low for now. Is there anywhere else you can hide out in the meantime?"

"Julianne has the key to a cabin that belongs to her neighbor," David said. "It's outside the state park area off Sangchris Lake." He gave Mack the details Julianne had given him on the way to Joliet. "I can't promise you it's safe, but it doesn't have any connection to us in particular."

"The neighbor would know you were there," Mack reminded him.

"Julianne told her she didn't have vacation time yet at her job,"

David said. "I don't know where she thinks Julianne's gone at this point, but there's no reason for her to assume she's heading there."

"But she would know Julianne was gone?"

"I believe so," David replied. "The lady's the motherly type, bringing over food and that sort of thing. Her son lives with her, and he seems to have a crush on Julianne."

"Great," Mack said.

"Somebody poisoned the neighbor's dog to keep it quiet the night before we left."

"Why?"

"Best I can tell, he wanted to assess the house to see if I was in there," David said. "If you want, have them checked out. Mrs. Rhoda Spielmann and her son, Larry. They live next door to Julianne."

"I'll see what we can find on them," Mack said. "For now, what are we going to do about you two? You should have picked somewhere besides Farrar's place to get rid of him. You should have expected more of Fulton's guys to be around."

"He didn't give me any other choice," David responded. "I wanted to find out what he knew about Julianne and what they had planned for her. When he shot me, he thought I was dead. He would have told Paul about me anyway, and Paul would have told his father."

"They must have sent somebody to watch Julianne after that," Mack said. "Or they've been watching her all along."

"They set up that job and the house so they could keep an eye on her," David said. "Either they already knew I wasn't dead, or there's something they want from her. What was in that box you gave her at my funeral?"

"What do you mean?" Mack asked, sounding surprised. "I didn't hand her anything important. It was your personal stuff from the office.

The contents of the box had nothing to do with any of our investigations. If they did, why would I give them to Julianne?"

"I don't know," David said. "Did you examine everything before you gave her the box?"

"Becker and I went through that stuff before I passed it on," Mack answered, referring to Ted Becker, a fellow FBI agent. "We had to make sure there wasn't anything sensitive in there. We even examined the notebook with all your video game notes to see if you had added anything else that might apply to the case."

"Maybe I'm worried over nothing," David said. "We left the stuff from the box at Julianne's house anyway. Everything except the box itself and the little rug."

"Did you check them out?" Mack asked.

"Of course I did," David answered. He described the box and the rug. "I didn't notice anything unusual about either of them. I can bring them in if you want. Maybe somebody at the bureau can figure out if there's anything special about them."

"No," Mack snapped.

David winced at his friend's sharp tone. "What's going on? You know something."

"I don't know anything for sure," Mack said, his voice calmer but still full of tension. "Like I told you, Becker was the one who helped me pack the box. He said those things were all your personal property, but maybe he knew something different."

"Do you think that rug was something he could have put in the box deliberately?" David asked. He left the bed and retrieved the rug and the flattened box it had been in. Neither of them seemed the slightest bit out of the ordinary. The box was a simple box, and the rug was cheap and garish. "Or maybe they're interested in the box. You should ask Becker about it."

"I can't ask him," Mack said. "He's dead."

"What?" David asked, stunned. "How did that happen?"

"He was shot down in front of his house two weeks after your funeral," Mack answered. "It was a drive-by, and it happened right in front of his wife and kids."

"Oh no," David breathed. "Do you think Fulton has somebody in the bureau?"

"Apparently he does," Mack said. "I don't know who, but it must be somebody close to the case. Paul's still running the money-laundering business for his father. What you were in on shut down part of it and put Mike Fulton behind bars, but everything else is still functional. We've been trying to nail him on all of it, but so far everything we've investigated is totally aboveboard."

"But they're still after me," David pointed out.

"I'm sure of it." Mack paused for a second. "Listen, maybe they're not after anything in the box. It's possible they wanted to flush you out of hiding, and making things hot for Julianne would be a guaranteed way of getting your attention."

"That's what I was guessing." David sighed. "Now what do we do?"

"Get to that cabin on the lake, and stay out of sight. I'll send somebody to you. There's only one of our agents who couldn't possibly be involved with Fulton."

"Only one?" David asked, alarmed.

"I'm not saying our whole unit is bad," Mack said, "but I'm not sure who is and who isn't except in this one instance."

"Who should I watch for?" David asked.

"If somebody strikes up a conversation with you and complains about being transferred to Savannah, you need to mention that you have a brother who moved to Savannah with his wife and their dog."

"Is that all?"

"If you're asked what the dog's name is, pick a name that starts with the same letter as whichever day of the week it happens to be," Mack said. "Got it?"

"Yeah, sure."

"The other person will tell you about having as many dogs as whatever hour of the day it happens to be," Mack said.

"The dog's name starts with whatever letter the day of the week starts with, and the other guy has as many dogs as the hour of the day," David summarized.

"That's right," Mack said. "But—"

Over the phone line, David heard a loud knock. It sounded like someone was at Mack's door.

"But what?" David asked.

"I have to go," Mack said, his voice barely audible. "Someone's here. Call me back when you can."

Before David could say anything else, the line went dead.

Julianne came out of the bathroom, dressed and as reasonably fresh as she could manage on the tiny bit of sleep she'd had that night.

David stood by the bed, frowning. The little rug was spread out on the comforter, and the flattened cardboard box was next to it.

"Was that Mack?" she asked, joining him. "I heard you talking."

"Yeah," he said, sounding distracted.

Julianne waited for him to elaborate. When he didn't say anything else, she asked, "What did he tell you?"

"Mack thinks somebody from our unit might have sold out to Fulton," David answered.

"That's terrible," she said, putting a hand over her heart. "What do we do?"

"He's going to send the only person he can trust to help us," David said.

"Who is it?" Julianne asked.

He shrugged and flipped the rug over, studying it. "Mack told me how to recognize the agent through code words, but he didn't have a chance to tell me who it was. Someone knocked on the door, and he had to go. I'm supposed to call him back. I'll give him a little while to get rid of whoever it was before I try again."

"Where are we supposed to go now?" she asked. "Is he lining up a place for us?"

"Mack doesn't have a safe place at the moment," David said. "He told me to drive to the cabin and stay out of sight."

She nodded, grateful that they finally had their next step.

"How about we get some real breakfast?" David asked. "We don't know how the day's going to go, so we should have at least one good meal. It might have to last the rest of the day or even longer."

She wasn't hungry enough for a big meal, but they needed to eat when they had the chance. It might be a long time before they had another hot breakfast.

"I paid for three nights here," Julianne reminded him. "Do you think we can get a refund?"

"I doubt it. You paid cash, and this motel is pretty seedy," David said. "Don't worry. We have enough money. Let's go."

They packed their belongings, loaded them into the car, and drove away from the motel. Soon they stopped at an out-of-the-way diner. David ordered bacon, scrambled eggs, oatmeal, and coffee.

Julianne shook her head, wishing she had his hearty appetite, but she ended up ordering a Denver omelet, a bowl of oatmeal, and coffee. She had never imagined that she would be running for her life, but it was what she had to do right now. There was no use denying it. All she could do was confront it head-on and try to see the bright side. She suddenly giggled.

David glanced up, a forkful of scrambled eggs halfway to his mouth. "What's so funny?"

"I was attempting to put a positive spin on all this, and I realized that at least I won't have to file office correspondence today."

"I'm sorry I got you into this mess," he said softly.

"I am too," she admitted. "But it's where we are. I'm coming to terms with the fact that there's nothing to do now but get out of it the best we can."

"We'll get out of it together." David smiled and reached across the table for her hand. "We've always made a great team."

Feeling her pulse suddenly race, Julianne grabbed her spoon and took another bite of oatmeal.

He picked up his coffee cup and drained it. "I'll try Mack again when we get out to the car. Then we can head to the cabin, okay?"

"You're the one who's trained for this kind of thing. I have no idea what we should do at this point." She stared down at her plate for a moment. "I trust you to take care of us. I'm not sure if I'm still mad at you, but there's no use dwelling on it now. The whole idea of who's right or wrong and why doesn't mean anything if we end up dead."

David didn't say anything, but his eyes were full of relief and determination and love.

"I don't know what might happen between us after this is over," Julianne said firmly. "But we're in this together, and I'll do what you think is best." When she searched his face, she noticed a flicker of pain.

"That's a good start anyway," he said. "And I promise I'll do whatever I have to do to keep you safe."

Once they'd finished eating and paid the check, they exited the restaurant and walked to the car.

"Why don't you try to get some sleep?" David suggested as he slid behind the wheel. "You didn't get much rest last night."

"I'm all right now that I'm awake," she told him. "The coffee really helped."

"Let me call Mack, and we'll get going." He removed his phone from his pocket and dialed.

Julianne heard the phone ring four times before it went to voice mail. She glanced at David. He narrowed his eyes, watching the traffic passing by. Julianne was sure that he was on alert for any sign they were being followed.

He ended the call without leaving a message. Then he dialed again. There was still no answer. David started the car and pulled out into the street. He stopped long enough to buy three more burner phones and dump the one he had just used into the trash behind a drive-through chicken restaurant.

"What now?" she asked.

"I need to go to Mack's house," David said. "I'm not sure he'll be there, but I have to check. He told me to call him back, so he should have been waiting for me."

"I thought we were going out to the cabin," Julianne said.

"First I have to find out what's going on with Mack. He thinks Fulton might have somebody in our unit. If that's the case, he's not safe and neither are we." He glanced at her, his lips pressed into a tight line. "I'm sorry I can't tell you in detail what we're going to have to do. Even if we made an elaborate plan, it could change at any second. Sometimes things can't be safe and predictable, no matter how much we'd like them to be."

"You mean how much *I'd* like them to be," she said, her tone sharper than she'd intended.

"You've always been more cautious than I am," David said. "Most of the time, you're right. That's one of the ways we balance each other out. Sometimes you're too worried about planning out every single thing, and sometimes I don't plan enough." A touch of humor softened his expression. "Mack tells me that even more than you do, if you can believe it."

Julianne frowned. What other potentially fatal scrapes had David been in the past few years when she'd foolishly believed he was doing routine audits for the IRS? How many times had he come home from a so-called seminar too tired to do much more than fall into bed and sleep for twelve hours straight? How many times had she believed he was being romantic when he'd walked through the door and immediately taken her into his arms, holding her close as if he'd been afraid he would never see her again?

"Anyway," he said, turning the car northwest, away from the cabin, "Mack's house isn't far from here. He might suspect his phone is bugged, and that's why he's not picking up. But I need to talk to him soon."

Julianne had just told him that she trusted him to take care of them, so she didn't try to talk him out of it, but why did they have to head toward trouble instead of away from it?

"How far away is he?" she asked.

"Half an hour, maybe a little more depending on traffic," David said. "It shouldn't take long."

Julianne leaned back in her seat, briefly closing her eyes. She believed that God guided the steps of those who trusted Him. If she was where He wanted her to be, wasn't she perfectly safe? And could she ever be safe anywhere else?

Please show me, she prayed silently. *Show us both what to do.*

They drove for a few minutes without speaking.

"When we talked about the fire, you told me that you weren't home," he said, breaking the silence. "Where were you?"

"I was at work. If you say the fire was deliberately set, then they must have been watching the house to see when I left." She bit her lip, trying to keep the unsteadiness out of her voice and knowing she wasn't successful. "Do you think they burned down the house to get rid of whatever they think I have?"

"I don't know," David said. "When they found out I was alive, I assumed that threatening you was their attempt to get me to come out of hiding. They were right. I believed I was protecting you by going alone, but I really put you more in harm's way."

"It's not your fault," Julianne said, and she knew it was true. "You could have stayed where you were, avoiding the risk of them finding you again. The fact that you didn't do that shows that you care about me."

"No matter what it takes, I'm going to get us out of this," he said firmly. "I promise you I will."

Tears filled her eyes, and she blinked them away. She would look weak and foolish if she cried. She remained silent as she kept her gaze on the road in front of them.

"I've been thinking about your paintings," he said. "I'm sorry you lost them. They were amazing, and I know how much time and effort you put into them."

"I have to admit it was difficult seeing them destroyed." Julianne sighed. "Even the pictures I took of them are gone."

"Maybe you can paint them again someday," David suggested.

She shook her head, remembering how much she'd learned by painting each one, how brushstroke by brushstroke she had created a piece of art that was somehow more than she had envisioned.

"They would never be the same," Julianne admitted. "I'm not the same. When I painted them, I was at a different place in my life and skills. Even if I tried to reproduce them, they would reflect the way I see them now, not the way they originally were."

"That might not be a bad thing," he said.

"If I picked up a paintbrush, I would want to do something completely different. The subject would have to mean something to me now." She shrugged. "But I don't see myself ever painting again."

"Why in the world not?" David asked, sounding startled. "You're a great artist. People just haven't realized it yet."

Julianne waved away his comment. "You always say that."

"Because it's true."

She was surprised to feel heat come into her cheeks. "There's no accounting for taste."

"You don't know what you could have done if you'd let yourself," David said. "If you had studied art instead of information systems."

"You realize 'starving artist' is a saying for a reason, right?"

"None of the artists who made it were successful because they didn't try," he countered.

"I never wanted to be famous," Julianne said. "I like to paint. I mean, I used to like it."

"You don't like it anymore?"

"Lately I haven't had much time to think about it," she said.

David raised one eyebrow. "Because of your hectic work schedule or your packed social calendar?"

Julianne glared at him. He knew that she had a job that required very little of her. He probably also knew that her social life had been practically nonexistent since he'd left. Whose fault was that? No, she wasn't going there. She wasn't going to blame him for it. Besides, it didn't matter. Neither did this particular conversation.

"Look," she said, "I don't know what that has to do with anything right now."

"Honestly, I wanted to hear more about what you've been doing since I've been gone," he said. "I hate to think if something did happen to me that you would stop doing what makes you happy. If you want to paint, you should paint."

"That's the problem," Julianne said. "I don't know if I still want to paint."

"Whatever God puts inside you is what you're made to do," David said. "If it's painting, then it'll be a shame if you don't do it anymore. It'll be a real loss to you and everybody around you and a waste of God's gift. But you know that already. Isn't that why you told me I should join the Marines instead of staying in college to please my dad?"

"Yeah, I suppose," she said. "But sometimes doing what we want to do isn't the wisest decision."

He blew out a breath. "Some people need to stand up to the criminals."

"Yes, they do." Julianne truly loved David's courage and protectiveness. He was the most dedicated man she'd ever known. "I just wish that everything you wanted to do wasn't so dangerous."

"I didn't intend for it to be this dangerous," he said. "At least not for you."

"What happens to you affects me," she argued. "Do you have any idea what it felt like when they told me you were dead?"

"I've tried to tell you that it was the only way to protect you," David said. "At least I thought it was."

"No, that's not what I'm saying," Julianne replied. "Perhaps it was the best thing to do at the time. But from the moment you took that assignment, you were putting your life at risk. You could have been killed at any minute."

"You don't have to remind me," he said. "I should have trusted you and talked to you about the position before I accepted it. I guess I didn't want to worry you. I'm sorry. I hope you can someday forgive me for everything I've put you through."

As Julianne studied David, she desperately wanted to forgive him. But how?

Davis drove them to a quiet neighborhood west of where they'd spent the night.

"Mack lives in one of those huge apartment complexes," he said. "Nobody usually pays attention because people are coming and going all the time. Lots of different cars around."

"What's the plan?" Julianne asked.

"Mack's place is in the rear," David said. "There's an alley that goes behind the whole building that leads right past his garage door."

She raised her eyebrows. "You can get into his garage?"

"Probably not," David admitted. "I'll climb to the roof and get to his balcony from there. I did it once during a different case we were working together."

"Don't tell me about it," Julianne responded. "The last thing I want to hear right now is how many other times you've nearly been killed."

"There's a car repair shop at the end of the block," he said, returning the conversation to the task at hand. "I'm going to get out of the car at the coffee shop next door to it. You take the car to the repair shop and tell them it's making a weird sound and you need it checked out."

"Should I wait at the repair shop?" she asked.

"Yes," David said. "I'll be back before they even get it into the bay. If for some reason they get a chance to inspect it and tell you nothing's wrong, describe something that's going to be hard for them to evaluate quickly. You'll think of something."

He knew that Julianne would have no trouble making up a problem.

She had once told him that her dad had made sure his daughters knew enough about their cars to avoid being taken advantage of by repairmen.

She nodded.

"Take a phone," David said, handing her one. "When I'm through talking to Mack, I'll call you. Tell the repair shop you can't wait any longer, then pick me up at the end of the alley. What do you think?"

"That doesn't sound too hard," she remarked as she pocketed the phone.

"Act natural," he said. "It's normal if you seem a little nervous. They'll assume you're worried about the car. You'll be safe there, but sit away from the windows if you can."

"How long do you think you'll be gone?" Julianne asked.

"I'll be back as soon as I can," David said as he slid the gun into his pocket. "Stay as much out of sight as you can, and pray that Mack's at home."

"What if he isn't?" she asked.

David hoped he wouldn't have to worry about that. "Then I'll try to call him again and figure out where he is."

He drove the short distance to the coffee shop. It had a striped awning over the front, and a few people sat outside at the small tables, sipping their coffee.

David pulled into a parking space at the side of the building and exited the car.

She walked around the vehicle and got into the driver's seat. "Be careful," she told him.

He wanted to lean down and kiss her and tell her everything would be all right, but he figured that neither the words nor the gesture would be welcome. Instead, he patted the gun in his pocket. "I'll be back soon."

David stood in the parking space until Julianne drove to the repair shop and stopped in the shade of some trees. He watched her climb out of the car and go inside the building. He was glad the front windows had been tinted to dim the heat of the sun. It was hard to tell who was inside while driving by. She was safe for the time being.

He went into the coffee shop and bought a cup of the house blend, then walked farther down the block to the alley that ran behind Mack's building. The alley was deserted. It was a workday, so he didn't expect to see anyone. If he ran into somebody, he planned to say that he was searching for a lost cat.

David strolled down the alley, sipping his coffee and pretending to check the trees and under bushes for the supposed cat. A dog barked at him from a window, but David only glanced its way. He doubted anyone was home.

Despite his leisurely pace, it didn't take long to arrive at Mack's. David tossed his coffee cup into the trash bin behind the building, then climbed a wide-spreading oak that allowed him to drop onto the garage roof and make his way over to his friend's balcony. They were more like town houses than apartments, though he didn't think Mack owned his outright. They each had a small garage and a miniature backyard. They shared common walls, but each unit was three stories high. David was glad he didn't have to worry about upstairs or downstairs neighbors spotting him. The alley ran alongside a creek and a wide band of trees, so no one would be able to see him from behind the building either.

Before David had been forced to disappear, he had worked closely with Mack, often using Mack's house when he needed a safe place to stay. He still had a key, and he used it now, silently opening the French doors that led to Mack's bedroom.

Gun in hand, he scanned the room, but it was empty. The bed wasn't made, and there were a few articles of clothing wadded up on the floor, but the room was otherwise tidy, sleek, and contemporary. No frills or fuss. Lots of electronics. That was Mack.

Maybe Mack wasn't home after all. If he was, he was likely downstairs in his office. David thought for a moment that it was too quiet in the house, and then he heard the heavy scrape of a large piece of furniture being moved. He took a few steps and made sure there was no one in the bathroom or the closet.

David edged to the bedroom doorway, listening closely. Whoever was downstairs was searching for something, pulling out drawers and rifling through cabinets. The person obviously assumed he was alone to make so much noise. Mack had to be out.

He slipped out of the bedroom and over to the wall across from it. The living room was two stories high, and the upstairs hallway overlooked it. He crept to the end of the wall, sank down to one knee, and peered through the railing, trying to glimpse what was going on downstairs.

The intruder was evidently tearing apart the kitchen. David could hear the rattle of the silverware drawer as it was yanked open and slammed shut. From the sound of it, the guy was even checking the appliances.

For a few minutes, David listened, debating whether he should go downstairs and confront the intruder or wait and see what else was going on. Remembering Julianne was waiting for him, he stayed where he was, crouched behind the wall, watching.

Still hearing banging and clattering in the kitchen, David leaned forward a bit more. He could see the tan leather sectional sofa now. It was set up in the middle of the room, and it faced the front windows. Mack was sitting on the couch, his head resting on his arm, which was draped over the back of the cushions. He was motionless, and his shirt was soaked with blood.

Horrified, David gaped at the scene.

Mack was dead.

14

David couldn't believe that Mack had been murdered.

Before he could do anything, the intruder strode into the living room. He was slim and elegant, impeccably groomed, and dressed in an expensive suit.

David did a double take at the man. It was Cameron Porter, Mack's new partner. David had met him briefly at the office, and he knew he had been assigned to take David's place as Mack's partner after his supposed death.

"Where is it?" Porter demanded of Mack's body. He growled a curse, then snatched Mack up by his shirtfront and threw him onto the coffee table.

Mack slid awkwardly to the floor, ending up on his back and staring at the high ceiling with unseeing eyes.

Even though David had already known he was dead, he flinched.

David clenched his pistol. Porter was a traitor and a murderer. He'd killed Mack. He deserved death. Still, that wasn't David's decision to make. All David could do was hold him for the police. But that was all right as long as Porter didn't walk away from this.

David stood and aimed his gun at Porter's sleek head, anticipating the look of astonishment that would be in the assassin's eyes when he realized he was no longer alone. David almost hoped that Porter would attempt to make a break for it, giving him no choice but to shoot. He almost hoped—

The front door flew open, and David pressed his back against the wall.

A muscular man in a dark suit stormed inside. He was no doubt another one of Fulton's men. "Anything?"

Porter gestured toward Mack's body. "He went for his gun before I could get anything out of him. You'd better bring in the rest of your men. We'll have to tear the place apart."

David quietly inched into the bedroom and slipped out the French doors. Swiftly and silently, he crossed the garage roof and swung down from the tree.

Once he was clear, he sprinted down the alley and ducked into a nearby grocery store. He wandered through the aisles for a few minutes, letting his breathing slow to normal as much as possible, trying to seem at least mildly interested in the items in the bargain section.

Finally, David picked up two different brands of glass cleaner and studied them both. Then he pulled out his phone and called Julianne. "Hey, honey," he said even before she spoke. "I'm at the grocery store."

"The grocery store?" Julianne echoed.

"Yeah, the one across from the repair shop," David said. "I was getting the glass cleaner, but I wasn't sure which brand to get. Any preference?"

"Do you need me to pick you up?" she asked. "I'm still waiting for them to check out the car."

"You'd better come now," he replied. "We can get the glass cleaner later. I'll be watching for you."

"Be right there," she said and hung up.

As David purchased a newspaper and a bag of red licorice, he pictured Mack in his living room and winced. He couldn't believe that his friend was gone. Why had Porter killed him? What was he searching for? And what would David and Julianne do now?

He pushed the bleak thoughts away and went outside to meet her.

Julianne's stomach roiled with nerves as she pulled up in front of the grocery store.

Before she could come to a complete stop, David appeared at the front passenger door. He yanked it open and jumped inside. "Go," he said as he buckled his seat belt, his expression calm.

People who didn't know David well might not have noticed that his expression was forced, but she did. Julianne's anxiety heightened, and she wondered what had happened.

"Don't make it seem like you're in a hurry," he instructed.

Julianne took her time driving away from the store. When they arrived at a stoplight, she glanced at him and asked, "Which way?"

David didn't appear to be hurt, but there was a grimness in his expression that hadn't been there when she'd dropped him off at the coffee shop. He'd found something at Mack's place. Or Mack had given him bad news. Or they were in more trouble than either of them had suspected.

"Go out the way we came in, and get back on the highway." His words were tight and clipped, his hands clenched into fists.

She didn't say anything for a few more minutes. "What happened?" she finally asked, bracing herself.

"Mack's dead."

"Oh no!" Julianne gasped. "I'm so sorry."

"Me too." David turned his head so he was facing the side window. "He was a good guy. A good agent."

"It sounds like you were close." She considered how much of David's life he'd spent on a job she never even knew about until recently. How many cases had he and Mack worked on together? How many times had they risked their lives to track down and arrest criminals? "Did he have a family?"

"Yes, but his wife left him last year and took their two kids," he said. "Mack only saw them once in a while."

Julianne winced. She wondered if Mack had kept his work in the FBI a secret like David had. Or had Mack's wife left him because of his dangerous job? Julianne decided not to ask what happened.

"I desperately wanted to take out the guy who killed him," David said, his voice cracking.

Fear pulsed through her, and her heart started to race. "You saw his murderer?"

"He was standing right there in Mack's living room," he answered. "I had my gun pointed at his head. Nobody would have questioned it if I'd shot him. I should have shot him."

"Why didn't you?" Julianne knew the answer, but she wanted to hear him say it.

David scowled. "Even Porter's supposed to have a trial, and executions aren't in my job description." His expression suddenly softened. "And I knew you were waiting for me. I didn't want to start something that might get traced back to us. Back to you."

She merged onto the highway, picking up speed. "He didn't see you?"

"No, but someone else arrived," he said. "He was probably one of Fulton's men. Porter told him to call in some other guys to search the place. I can't say whether that has to do with us, and now I don't know who to contact about it."

"What about the agent Mack told you about?" she asked. "The one he trusted. Can he help us?"

"I don't have a clue who the agent is or how to get in touch with him," David answered. "I know some code to identify him, but that's about it. I'm afraid we're on our own."

Dread filled Julianne, and a lump formed in her throat. She'd been clinging to the hope that once they reached Mack, he would usher them to safety. Now her hope was shattered. "Do you think the cabin is still safe?"

"You don't have to worry about Mack telling anyone about it," he said. "He wouldn't have done that. He knew Fulton had gotten to somebody in our unit, but he didn't have a name. Mack probably didn't even realize who it was until Porter put a bullet in his heart."

"So, who's Porter?" she asked. "Do you know him?"

"He was assigned as Mack's new partner after I disappeared," David said. "I met him at the office. From what I understand, he's been an agent for a long time. I couldn't say whether he was a plant from the very beginning or if Fulton's guys got to him later. They might have something on him, or maybe they picked up somebody important to him."

"Do you mean a hostage?" Julianne asked, her dread intensifying. "Somebody in his family?"

"It's possible, but I'm simply guessing at this point," he said. "Whatever the reason, Porter sold out. He killed Mack."

"Do you think Porter knew all along that you were alive?" she asked.

David paused, and she could feel the pain and anger radiating from him. "I'm not sure."

"Who else would have known about you besides Mack?"

"Some of the higher-ups in the bureau," he replied. "Mack was my contact. Nobody in my unit was supposed to be in on it, but if somebody leaked that I was alive, it would have been recently. If Fulton wants to get rid of me so badly, they wouldn't have waited five months to find me. Unless . . ."

She glanced over at him. "Unless what?"

"Porter was searching for something at Mack's," David said. "That's why he was planning to tear up the house."

"I'm confused," Julianne admitted. "I thought they were sure that you had it."

"So did I," he said. "But they might think that was a decoy, and Mack still has the real thing."

Sudden anger flared inside her. "What do you mean? That all this has been a ruse? That we could have been killed over nothing?"

"I don't think so," David said. "Whether or not we have anything Fulton is searching for, he wants me dead. I tried my best to get to Mack and find out more, but I didn't make it. I blew it, and now he's gone."

Her anger cooled. "It's not your fault."

"Isn't it?"

"No, it's not," Julianne said firmly. "If you'd gotten there a few minutes earlier, Porter would have simply killed you too. You aren't responsible for what a criminal does."

David didn't respond.

"And it's not your fault what happened with Fulton and his people before," Julianne continued. "You did your job, and you're right that somebody has to stand up to men like them." She bit her lip. "I wish you'd been honest with me about the whole thing."

"I realize that," he said, "and I'm sorry."

She didn't need another apology from him. Apologies couldn't make it okay, and the best intentions couldn't do anything to fix this horrible situation. It was done.

With that, she knew that even if David hadn't been honest with her, she had to be honest with him.

"I know you are," Julianne said evenly. "I understand it didn't turn out like you planned. I believe you were trying to protect me, and I appreciate it. I want you to be safe, and I'll help you however I can, but that's all I can do."

David stared at her. "What are you saying?"

"I can't be married to you anymore," she answered, avoiding his gaze. "I'm not sure if we're still legally married anyway."

He didn't say anything.

"We've been married for seven years, and you've lied to me the whole time." Julianne gripped the steering wheel so hard her knuckles turned white. "I can't believe how gullible I was. I should have asked more questions about your job and met your supervisor and coworkers. I blindly trusted you when you told me you were working on some projects for the government that you couldn't give me much information about."

"That was true," David said with soft resignation.

"You said it was related to the IRS," Julianne reminded him. "Not criminal investigations that would put both of our lives at risk." She glared at him. "Did it even cross your mind that we could be killed because of your job?"

"No," he said. "I thought I was protecting you. I was doing everything I could to stop this from happening. I'm sorry."

"Don't tell me how sorry you are." She silently counted to ten. "I'm trying to deal with this situation. Granted, I'm not doing it very well, but I'm trying."

"You are doing well, especially considering what I've put you through," David said. "I know this isn't easy."

Julianne couldn't keep a touch of bitterness out of her sudden laugh. "I should have listened to Dannie when she tried to warn me that something was going on with you."

"She thought I was having an affair," he responded.

"Even Dannie wouldn't have suspected that you were a secret agent," she said. "If I had listened to her, at least I would have confronted you about it, and then you would have told me what you were involved in."

He exhaled. "I don't know what else to say."

They drove in silence until the low fuel light popped on.

"We need gas," Julianne announced as she veered into the right lane.

"There's a station at the next exit," David said, pointing. "Do you want me to take over the driving?"

"I could use a break." She took the exit, then steered into the gas station lot and pulled up next to a pump.

He gave her a few bills, and she went inside the station to pay.

When Julianne returned to the car, David was pumping gas. She got into the passenger seat and buckled herself in, watching as the wind tugged at the loose curls on top of his head. His hair was darker, but otherwise he looked the same. Maybe he was a little leaner than before. Had he missed her? He claimed he had. She had no reason not to believe him, but did she have any reason to believe him?

Lord, please help me. What am I going to do?

He reentered the car. "Ready to go?"

Julianne wasn't ready, but what choice did she have? There was no going back, not for either of them. She nodded.

David drove away from the gas station and merged onto the highway.

They were silent as the minutes ticked by. Julianne couldn't stop thinking about Mack and the family he'd left behind. Her heart broke for them. It was such a tragedy.

"Are we going to drive all the way to the lake without talking?" he asked, glancing at her.

"I don't know what to say right now," she admitted. "I keep thinking about what happened to Mack."

"Me too," David said, his voice low and husky.

"I feel terrible for his wife and children," Julianne went on. "Did his wife know about his job?"

"He told her before they got married," he answered. "I guess it wasn't until they had kids that his job really bothered her. She said it was too dangerous. What was Mack supposed to do about that?"

"Maybe pick a different job," she said sharply. She instantly regretted it.

"It's hard on the families," David said. "I don't have to tell you that. I didn't want to get you in trouble. That was something I always tried to avoid. Even if you don't love me anymore, I'm still going to do my best to get you somewhere safe and keep you safe."

"I never said I don't—"

"You don't have to say it," he interrupted. "I'm not asking you to make any kind of decision right now, but I want you to know that anybody who's after you will have to come through me first. I promise you that, okay?"

"Okay," Julianne whispered, then turned to gaze out the side window.

She didn't tell him she still loved him, though she knew she did and always had. She didn't tell him that she couldn't keep on living this way either. He'd had enough to deal with for one day. What happened later didn't matter. For now, they had to get to the cabin.

At the cabin, they would finally be safe.

David drove up to the tiny cabin at the end of a dirt road that seemed more like a deer trail. "Here we are," he announced as he shifted the car into park.

Julianne unbuckled her seat belt and reached for the door handle.

"Wait a minute," he said, stopping her. "Let me check things out before we go in."

"Do you think someone's here?" she asked, her eyes wide.

"No, but I need to be absolutely sure." David slipped his gun into his pocket. "Do you have the key?"

Julianne rummaged around in her purse, retrieved a little wire ring with a rusted key, and handed it to him.

"Lock the doors," he instructed. "If anybody shows up, you take off. Deal?"

"Leave you here?" she asked. "I can't do that."

"It's a precaution," David said. "Just promise, all right?"

Julianne nodded.

"Keep your eyes open," he said. "If you see anything, honk the horn and then take off. I'll be back in a minute."

David and Julianne exited the car, and she got into the driver's seat.

He waited until he heard the distinct click of the locks before pulling his gun and striding toward the old cabin. It was a cheaply constructed building that had seen better days. He trudged through knee-deep weeds to one of the side windows and peeked inside. The curtains were drawn, but he could see through a little gap in the middle.

The cabin appeared to be empty. There was one main room that served as the living room and bedroom, and it featured a couch that made a bed, an end table, and a chest of drawers. On the wall across from him were three doors. They most likely went to the kitchen and bathroom, and the last one was probably a closet. Judging from the outside, they were all very small.

David walked around to the rear of the cabin and found the door locked and the curtains completely closed. As he stepped onto the creaky covered porch, he gripped the battered railing, but he let it go when it moved unsteadily in his hand. It was obvious that no one had done any maintenance out here in a long time.

There was a wooden box, like a chest, that was built beside the back door against the side of the house. The box was sheltered by the roof overhang and ventilated on both sides. It had a latch on it with a loop for a padlock, but there was no lock on it. David carefully lifted the lid and noticed the end of a power cord sticking out of the wall, the plug obviously intended for a generator. On the far side of the cabin, there was only one window, and it was frosted for privacy. He was sure that was the bathroom.

David returned to the front of the cabin and climbed the steps to the door, pushing away a brown paper sack that had blown against it. He peered into the front window, where the curtain didn't quite cover it on one side. Scanning the room, he didn't notice anything to indicate that someone had been inside in at least several months.

With his gun still in hand, David unlocked the door and entered the cabin. He was met with solemn silence. In several quick strides, he was at one of the three doors. He threw it open and saw the bathroom. It contained a bathtub, a sink, and a toilet. The tub was empty. So was the closet except for the generator and the big box fan stored there. A thick layer of dust coated everything.

He flicked on the light switch in the bathroom, but nothing happened. He tried again in the living room with the same result.

In the kitchen were a few cabinets, a small table and two chairs, and a stove. There was no refrigerator. Julianne's neighbors probably ran the generator when they stayed here and used an ice chest to keep food fresh. That actually worked in his and Julianne's favor now. There was less chance that anyone would find them off the grid like this.

David hurried to the car, feeling at least slightly less wary than he had, and motioned for Julianne to unlock the doors.

She pressed the button.

"All clear," he said as he jumped into the passenger seat. "We need to pick up a few things, though."

Julianne frowned. "They told me it was already stocked."

"I didn't check the kitchen cabinets, so there might be some canned goods," David said. "But there's no refrigerator. We need an ice chest and ice and fuel for the generator. Plus, a few things to eat." He smiled. "We can't live on licorice."

"We passed a general store on the way in," she reminded him. "It's not far, and it should have what we need."

"Let's go," he said.

Julianne started the car and headed down the path to the store.

"We should figure out what to call ourselves if anybody asks," David said. "We definitely don't want to use Montgomery. Better not use Julianne and David either."

"How about Kit and Ray?" she suggested.

He grinned. "Your mom and my dad. I like it. And the last name?"

"Not something so common it sounds fake."

"Like Smith or Jones," David said.

"And nothing so unusual that it's memorable," she added.

He nodded. "Sherman? Bender? Clark?"

"I like Sherman," Julianne said. "Ray and Kit Sherman."

"That works," David said. "We need to establish a basic story in case someone makes small talk. So, why are we here?"

"We borrowed our friend's cabin," she replied. "We wanted some couple time to reconnect."

"We should be able to sell that easy enough," he said. "Keep in mind that the fewer details you provide, the less you'll have to remember and the more authentic you'll seem. Don't appear to be covering anything up, but don't offer too much information. You'll sound like you're trying to be convincing."

"I'll let you do most of the talking," Julianne said.

"No, that's the worst thing you could do," David said. "If you act like you're scared to talk, people might think I've kidnapped you or something. Be natural. Not too friendly, not too shy. It would be good to act slightly bored, but don't overplay it. Got it?"

"Got it," she said.

He detected a hint of wariness in her tone, and he hoped she would be able to pull it off. If they encountered any trouble, he needed her support.

Their lives depended on it.

David parked in front of the general store that was housed in a small whitewashed shack. A white wooden sign with *Tuesday's* in peeling black letters hung over the door.

Julianne followed David inside.

Scanning the store, he saw that no one else was around except for a petite woman sitting behind the register. Judging by her weathered face and permed gray hair, he estimated that she was at least seventy. But the woman's blue eyes were bright, and David suspected that she was as sharp as a tack.

The place was a holdover from the thirties or forties, and the only nods to modernity were the security cameras over the cash register and the flat-screen TV behind the counter. The picture on the TV was terrible. It was faded and smeared, and it froze at random intervals.

The clerk scowled at the television. "Stupid streaming," she muttered, exhaling a cloud of cigarette smoke. "Can't get any service way out here."

David approached the counter with Julianne on his heels.

The clerk narrowed her eyes. "You're new."

"Yes, we drove in a few minutes ago," David said with his most disarming smile. "We borrowed a cabin in the woods, and we found out it's not as well stocked as we were told."

"You want luxury," the woman rasped, "you go to a ritzy hotel in the city."

David chuckled. "Good point."

"We wanted to rough it a little," Julianne said with a smile, "but we didn't expect it to be quite so rough."

"You lovebirds on your honeymoon?" the woman asked, sounding mildly disgusted.

"No," David told her. "We've been married awhile, but we thought it would be a good idea if we got away somewhere."

"You know how it is when you're apart so much." Julianne sidled up to him, taking his arm. "It's important to take the time to reconnect."

"No," the woman said, "I don't know."

A tabby cat jumped up on the counter and meowed.

The woman stroked one blue-veined hand down the cat's back. "I've got Petey here, and that's all."

"Hey, Petey." David held out a hand, allowing the cat to sniff him. Then David scratched behind Petey's whiskers with one finger.

The cat immediately leaned into him and closed his eyes, purring.

"How's that, buddy?" David asked with a grin.

"Well, Petey's certainly taken to you," the woman said, her voice softening. "I always trust his judgment about strangers. My name's Ruby Truvay."

"Ruby Tuesday," David said. "Like the song."

"That's it." She smiled at last and took a deep drag of her cigarette. "I've been Ruby Tuesday since I was seventeen."

"It suits you." David scratched the bald spot in front of one of the cat's ears, earning another blissful purr. "Like Petey suits him." He grinned at Julianne. "He's so friendly. Doesn't he remind you of Andy?"

"Yes, he does," Julianne agreed as she stroked the cat. "Our sweet Andy passed away."

"I'm so sorry you lost your cat," Ruby said.

"It's been a little over a year," Julianne said. "I miss him."

David knew the sadness in his wife's eyes was no act. They should have gotten another cat when Andy died, but neither of them had liked the idea of replacing him. Now David was glad there wasn't a cat to worry about in this mess.

"It's hard, isn't it?" Ruby patted Julianne's arm. "Do you have another cat?"

Julianne shook her head.

"You'll know when the time is right," Ruby assured her. "There are plenty of cats that need a good home."

"Very true," Julianne murmured.

After that, Ruby became quite the chatterbox. She shared amusing stories about Petey's antics and told them about the latest project in her quilting group. She informed them that she'd inherited the general store from her grandfather and hadn't changed a thing other than the name. Then she described the different items available for sale.

"If you need it, we've got it," Ruby said with a sly grin and her cigarette dangling from the corner of her mouth. "As long as you don't need much."

Julianne laughed.

"So," Ruby said, clasping her hands, "what do you folks need?"

David gave her a list, and Ruby helped them find everything on it, including food, ice, an ice chest, fuel for the generator, a gas can, and a battery-powered lantern.

As Ruby bagged their purchases, the door opened, and a man strode inside.

David went on high alert and swiftly sized up the newcomer. The man was tall and fit, and he wore a park ranger uniform. Despite the fading twilight, the man kept his mirrored sunglasses on. Clearly, the man didn't want anyone to read his eyes, and he was using it as a strategic advantage.

"Ms. Truvay," the ranger said, his voice low and emotionless.

"Evening," Ruby said, arching her eyebrows.

"Folks," the ranger said, addressing David and Julianne. "You staying the night?"

"We just arrived." David stuck out his hand. "Ray Sherman."

The ranger shook it. "Mr. Sherman."

"This is my wife, Kit," David said, smiling and gesturing to Julianne. He hoped she would continue to act natural.

The ranger nodded at her. "Ma'am," he said in that same emotionless voice.

"Nice to meet you," Julianne said.

The ranger faced David. "You didn't say how long you'll be staying at the lake."

No, I didn't, David thought, but he kept his smile firmly in place. "Oh, probably a few days. We haven't decided yet." He was sure the ranger was studying him, but all he could see was his own reflection staring back at him.

"You take care while you're with us," the ranger said.

"We'll do that," David said. He wanted to slip out before the ranger could ask any more questions, but he didn't want to appear to be in a hurry. He casually turned to Ruby. "What do we owe you?"

Ruby rang up their purchases and told him the amount.

David paid her with cash. "I think this will do for now. Thanks for everything, Ruby." He nodded at the cat. "Petey."

The cat meowed as if in response.

David and Julianne picked up the bags.

"Are you ready, Ray?" Julianne asked.

"Yeah, let's get going," David said. "See you, Ruby."

"You come back anytime," Ruby called after them.

David opened the door for Julianne, and they stepped out onto the front porch. Julianne seemed ready to bolt, so David caught her hand, slowing her down. When they reached the car, David opened the door for her and loaded the bags into the trunk.

As he walked to the driver's side door, he glanced at the general store. The ranger had followed them onto the porch. He was watching them.

David merely gave him a friendly wave before sliding behind the wheel and starting the car.

The ranger didn't acknowledge the wave. He stood for a moment longer on the porch, the scarlets and purples of the sunset reflected in his sunglasses. Then he went back inside.

On the short drive to the cabin, David and Julianne were silent, but he knew that she was as concerned about their encounter with the park ranger as he was.

When he stopped the car in front of the cabin, he faced her. "Don't worry. I'll check it out again before we settle in."

"That ranger freaked me out," she said. "Do you think he knows about us? Could he be after us?"

"Anybody could be after us," David said. "But there are a lot of cabins and cottages around the lake. He didn't follow us here, so it'll probably take him some time to figure out exactly where we are."

"How can I help if someone's inside waiting to kill you?" Julianne asked. "Or us?"

"It'll be okay," David assured her, and he hoped it was true. "Stay here and lock the doors until I secure the place."

She agreed, but she didn't seem convinced.

David took out his gun. He would have preferred to leave it with Julianne because she'd be safer with it, but only if she knew how to use it, and she had never wanted to learn. He walked to the front porch and unlocked the door.

After searching the entire cabin and the surrounding area, David found no evidence of an intruder. There were no new tire tracks on the path. Nothing seemed different since they'd gone to the store.

He returned to the car and got into the driver's seat. "It's all clear."

"Oh, good." Julianne sounded more than a little relieved.

"I'm going to park the car in the back," David said, turning the key in the ignition. "If someone finds us, it might not make much of a difference, but it could buy us enough time to escape."

There wasn't much of a clearing behind the cabin, but it was big enough to fit the car so it couldn't be seen from the front.

He exited the car and went to the trunk to unload their things. Julianne followed him.

"I don't want to light up the place," David said as he gathered the bags. He left the flattened box and the rug mixed in with the other emergency supplies in the trunk. "The curtains will definitely help to block the light."

"It's going to be warm inside," she remarked, grabbing a bag.

"It won't be too bad," he assured her. "Not at night anyway. We can open the curtains when the lights are out. For now, we can open the doors and windows to let in a nice breeze. There's a box fan if we need to use it, but I don't want to run the generator more than we have to."

As they carried the bags to the back porch, David motioned to the railing. "Watch out. It's pretty rickety."

Once they were safely inside, they set the bags down on the floor.

Julianne glanced around and chuckled. "Rhoda told me the cabin was cozy, but I didn't expect it to be this rustic."

"It'll be fine. We have everything we need." David locked the front and back doors, then stopped at each window to make sure the curtains were completely closed. Finally, he went to the bathroom cabinet, removed a navy-colored hand towel, and carried it to the kitchen.

"What's that for?" Julianne asked.

He rummaged around in one of the two drawers in the kitchen, found four thumbtacks, and showed them to her. "We need something to keep light from shining out of the bathroom window."

They walked into the bathroom.

David tacked the towel over the window, completely covering it. Then he opened the top of the toilet tank. "We'll have to refill the tank from the pump in the kitchen every time we flush."

She cringed. "No running water?"

"Sorry." He gave her a lopsided grin, hoping it would make her smile like it used to. "You're the one who wanted to come here."

"At least it's not an outhouse," Julianne said with a sigh.

"We won't be able to take regular baths," David added. "We would have to heat a lot of water for a bath, and we'd need to haul it to the tub and dump it out afterward."

"I guess we'll both live," she said with a small smile of her own.

"If we do this right, we will," he said.

Her smile vanished. "We can't stay here forever."

"No," he admitted. "I need to locate the agent Mack mentioned to me. I told Mack about this cabin, so he could have instructed our agent to contact us here. We'll have to wait and see."

"What about Mack's murderer?" Julianne asked. "Do you think anyone in the FBI knows who he is?"

"I'm not sure," David said. "I have to get word to the bureau about Porter in case they haven't identified him yet."

They returned to the kitchen.

"Can we make coffee?" she asked, motioning to a coffee maker on the counter.

He glanced at the machine. It was small and cheaply constructed, but it would brew two generous cups, and that was all they needed for now. "Sure. I'll fuel up the generator."

Julianne primed the kitchen sink with one of the bottles of water they'd brought along, and it took her a minute to get the pump going. "It would be a lot easier to wash out the coffeepot if I put it in the dishpan and ran water over it." As she turned on the water, she gasped. "Wow, it's freezing."

David smiled at her. "It's well water. Nice and cold." He retrieved the generator and the gas can and carried them to the back door. "Just a minute."

By the time he had the generator fueled and running, she had dried the coffeepot, set up the coffee maker, filled the appropriate reservoirs with water and coffee, and plugged it into the outlet near the window.

"Fire away," David said. He felt a certain satisfaction as he listened to the generator hum.

Julianne flipped the switch on the coffee maker, and it immediately started.

The enticing smell of the coffee intensified as it heated, filling the tiny room with soothing comfort.

They didn't need to unpack, but David sorted their belongings, storing the food in the kitchen and toiletries in the bathroom. He stowed their clothes in the old maple chest of drawers that stood against the front wall between the door and the window. At least they would be handy and out of the way.

That left the rug and the flattened cardboard box still in the trunk.

"We have to find a safe place for the rug and the box," David told her. "We still aren't sure if they're important or not, but we can't chance not taking care of them." He scanned the room, shaking his head. "I don't see a good hiding place."

"I suppose it wouldn't help to slip the rug inside one of the couch cushions," Julianne said. "If that's what they're actually trying to find."

"No, that's one of the first places they'll search."

"Why would anybody want the rug?" she asked, frowning. "It's cheap and ugly. Actually, it would be perfect for a place like this. People tend to dump their beat-up things from home in their weekend cabins."

"I don't know why they'd want it either," he said. "Is it even what they're after in the first place? I didn't notice anything special about it."

"I still wonder if it's a decoy," Julianne mused. "Maybe the trunk's the best place for it."

"For tonight anyway," David said. "It's already hidden out there with a bunch of other things. They might find it, but at least it'll take them longer."

The coffee maker beeped. Julianne found two chipped mugs in the cupboard and filled them. She handed one of the mugs to David, and they sat on the couch sipping their coffee.

David missed her so much that he could hardly stand it, but he knew she wasn't ready to talk about them as a couple. Not the couple that had been so happy together five months ago. Five short yet impossibly long months.

She placed her empty mug on the end table and met his eyes. "You told me you got Fulton sent to prison, but he's certainly gone to a lot of trouble to find you. Setting me up with my house and job would have taken a huge amount of planning. Will you tell me more about what happened?"

David would tell her what he could about what had happened. Nothing more. Not yet. "It was only a desk job, like I told you. At least at first." He ran one hand through his hair, suddenly wondering if she liked it so dark. "Then they asked me to do some undercover work. It wasn't supposed to be much, just enough to make Fulton's lieutenants feel comfortable while the real agents got the goods on them. But the old man liked me for some reason."

"Yes, you mentioned that he liked you," Julianne said. "I'm not surprised. You have a way with people, no matter who they are or what situation they're in. You've always been able to sweet-talk me into almost anything."

"I don't know about that," David said. He took the last sip of his coffee and set the mug aside. "I spent more than a year working at the bank, winning their trust, especially Fulton's. He never handled a transaction himself, and he never asked me to do anything illegal. He'd stop by my office and tell me about his grandkids and his boat and the horses he raced."

"So that's how you got to be friends," she murmured.

He nodded. "It was a very involved operation, and Mack was in charge of it. I had been set up as a loan officer in one of the major banks. I let it get out that I was in trouble financially, and Fulton's main guys paid me off to help launder a lot of money for them for a nominal fee. We worked together often."

"Didn't any of them suspect you?" Julianne asked.

"They were suspicious at first, but I got to know them and their families," David answered. "I was actually hanging out with them on some of the nights and weekends that I told you I had to work."

"I don't want to imagine you befriending criminals," she said.

"I didn't have to do it for long," he responded. "Soon Fulton invited me to his daughter's wedding. When I told Mack, he said it would be the perfect opportunity to round up Fulton's main guys because they'd all be in attendance."

"That's pretty cold, arresting people at a wedding," Julianne said.

Did he detect a hint of reproach? David shrugged. "Not compared to the kinds of things those men were doing. We weren't exactly trying to catch guys who didn't report their bingo winnings."

"You actually went to the wedding?" She put one hand over her mouth. "Now I remember hearing about it on the news. It was awful."

"Yes, I was there," David said grimly. "It didn't go as smoothly as we planned. A couple of our agents were killed, along with five of Fulton's men. One of them was the groom. Several other people were wounded.

We arrested eight of the eleven men we were after, including Mike Fulton himself. The other three were part of the group that got killed."

"I guess that explains why Fulton's after you." Julianne rubbed her eyes. "I still can't believe you got mixed up in all this."

"I was trying to do what was right and take down some very dangerous men," David said. "I don't even want to tell you the kinds of crimes Fulton and his guys committed. If you'd ever seen any of the people whose lives he's ruined, you'd want to do something too." He huffed in frustration. "He kills people like Mack. People like you. And it doesn't bother him one bit."

"I'm not saying somebody shouldn't have stopped him," she said. "But why did it have to be you?"

David reached over and took her hand. "I think I was meant to be where I was at that moment. To be honest, I didn't expect to be as involved as I was. Every minute I was terrified one of Fulton's men would see through me, but none of them ever did. It was like I was somehow protected every step of the way." He lifted her hand and touched his lips to it. "Like I'm going to protect you."

He knew he hadn't convinced her about that yet, but at least she didn't pull away.

When darkness fell, he turned off the generator and opened the front and back windows to let in the cool breeze.

David peered out the back window, watching and listening, but there was no sign of anyone coming their way. It was pitch-black out here away from the lights of civilization. The stars and the crescent moon seemed unnaturally close and bright, but not much of their light filtered down through the trees. He could barely see the outline of the car, but he caught the glint of moonlight reflected in the eyes of a creature in the woods. It was probably a deer. It wasn't a person, though. He was sure of that.

David rejoined Julianne on the couch, and they continued talking. This time, they didn't discuss Fulton or Mack or their current situation. Instead, they talked about everything that had happened to them while they'd been separated.

At first, David felt awkward, like telling his life story to someone he went to school with but hadn't seen in years. But the darkness made it more intimate with the singing of the crickets and the occasional hoot of an owl. It was the first time they'd really talked since he'd been gone.

During a lull in the conversation, David glanced at Julianne and noticed that her eyes were drifting shut. He was about to pull her closer to let her rest on his shoulder when he heard the crunch of tires on the dirt driveway and the low rumble of a car engine.

"Get behind the couch," he whispered as he pushed her down to the floor. "Hurry. Keep quiet."

Julianne scrambled behind the couch.

David removed the gun from his pocket and cocked it, then edged over to the windows. He hugged the wall as he stealthily shut and locked both windows. After making sure Julianne was hidden and the front door was locked, he crept to the back door and did the same.

He crouched in the darkness next to one of the front windows and waited. David set his jaw, determined to protect Julianne at any cost.

Even if it was his own life.

17

Julianne huddled behind the couch, fear seeping into her bones. She wanted to cry out when headlights flooded the room.

She couldn't move an inch to find out what was happening, but from where she was hunkered down, she could see David, gun in both hands, hiding in the shadows so he wouldn't be visible from outside.

The car stopped, and she heard the door open. Heavy footsteps thudded on the wooden steps and across the porch.

Her heart pounded, and she held her breath.

David was absolutely motionless, a part of the shadows, but Julianne could tell that he was ready to spring in order to protect her. She knew he would kill if he had to. She hoped it wouldn't come to that.

Please, Lord, no, she prayed, not daring to even whisper her petition. *Please.*

For a terrifying moment, there was only silence. Julianne was sure that whoever was on the porch was trying to see through the windows. Then the doorknob rattled.

She barely kept from screaming. *Please don't break in. Go away. Leave us alone.*

Every muscle tense, Julianne listened to the footsteps move away from the door and march from one window to the other. A few moments later, the person tramped down the porch steps and slammed the car door shut. Was the visitor really leaving?

She glanced at David. "Is he—"

"Shh!" he hissed. "Don't move."

The footsteps sounded on the porch again. They were stealthier this time. Once more, the doorknob rattled.

A phone rang, the sudden, piercing sound causing Julianne to flinch.

The intruder cursed, and his footsteps receded. The car door opened and closed again, and she heard the engine growl as it backed down the driveway.

She waited in the absolute silence for what felt like an eternity.

"We're clear," David finally announced. He stood and opened the windows, letting cool air into the stifling cabin. "Don't turn on any lights."

Julianne ran to him. "Did you see who it was?"

"No, I couldn't tell." He wiped away the glistening beads of sweat on his upper lip. "He was wearing dark clothes, glasses, and a hat pulled low."

"Do you think it was the ranger?"

"Possibly. He could have tracked us here. Or maybe he routinely checks these cabins."

"If it was routine, he wouldn't have left and come back, would he?" she asked.

"Probably not," David admitted. "We'll have to be extra careful."

"Perhaps we should get out," Julianne suggested, clinging to his arm. "There are other places we could hide."

"Not yet," he said. "Mack knew we were coming to this cabin, and he must have told the agent about it. So that person will expect us to be here. We have to wait."

She exhaled shakily.

David pulled her into his arms, holding her tightly. "Just for now," he murmured against her hair.

She nodded and stepped away from him.

David didn't say anything as he pulled a chair into the shadowy corner where he had huddled earlier.

Julianne knew he was going to stay up the rest of the night, keeping watch. She wished she could make him another cup of coffee, but they couldn't risk using the generator. Instead, she pumped two glasses of cold water.

"Why don't you get some rest?" David suggested. He sat down on the chair in the corner and downed the water.

Julianne drank her water and collapsed onto the couch. She had meant to pull out the hideaway bed, but she was too drained to move.

Before she drifted off to sleep, she whispered a prayer of gratitude.

Julianne woke at dawn when sunlight came through the windows.

David was still sitting in the chair in the corner. He held a cup of coffee, and the gun was on the floor by his feet. "Good morning," he said with an uncertain smile. "Did you sleep all right?"

Julianne had been curled up in one corner of the sofa with her head on the armrest. When she unfolded her arms and legs and straightened her shoulders, she ached all over. "As well as can be expected on this lumpy couch."

"Coffee?" he asked.

"That would be great." She ran one hand through her rumpled hair. "Did you sleep at all?"

"A little here and there." David shrugged. "I'm used to it."

Julianne was sure that he'd stayed awake all night standing guard. They went into the kitchen.

"I already made you a cup," David said, setting his mug on the counter. "I left the coffeepot on the burner, so it's still hot." He filled the other mug and handed it to her.

"Thanks," she said, taking a sip. It tasted wonderful. "Did you see anything else? Do you think we're safe here?"

"I think we're reasonably safe," he replied as they returned to the living area. "For the time being anyway. But we need to be careful. He could come back anytime."

Julianne shivered as she recalled the stranger's frightening visit last night. She hoped he wouldn't return.

"So, what do you want to do today?" David asked. He picked up his mug and took a drink.

She raised her eyebrows. It hadn't occurred to her that they'd be doing a lot of waiting. "You didn't bring a deck of cards, did you?"

"No, but we need to go back to the store anyway," he said. "I should have gotten extra batteries for the lantern. The ones it came with are already dying."

"Maybe we should get some batteries for the flashlight in the car too," Julianne said. "In case we need it."

"You haven't put new batteries in it before now?" David asked.

"You were always the one who took care of those things," she reminded him. "It was hard enough trying to tie up all the loose ends you left me with. I guess I missed one."

He put down his coffee cup and caught both of her hands.

When David hugged Julianne, she resisted, but then she realized she didn't want to. She was tired of resisting. She needed to feel his arms around her.

She put her arms around his waist and tucked her head under his chin. She'd missed the way they fit together as if they had been made for each other. Maybe they still were.

As David held her close, she soaked up the comfort of his warm and soothing embrace and the reality of him. David was alive. *Oh, God, thank You.*

Julianne thought she was going to cry, but instead she gazed up at him and managed a trembling smile. "There's a skillet in the cupboard. We could buy pancake mix." Pancakes were his favorite, and he used to tell her that she made the very best.

His eyes lit up. "I'll get my jacket."

She frowned slightly, pulling away from him. "It must be eighty degrees out there already. Why do you need your jacket?"

He picked up the gun, slid it into his waistband, and put on the jacket, which covered the weapon.

"I get it," Julianne said. "But you have to give me a chance to at least wash my face and brush my teeth."

"All right, slow down and finish your coffee," David said. "We've got nothing to do all day anyway."

"We need to do something," she said. "How long do you think we'll have to stay here?"

"We should be hearing from our contact before long. He'll get us somewhere safe."

"I can't believe there's no one else you can contact."

"I might have to take my chances and call someone else at the bureau," he said. "We have a burner phone we haven't used, but that gives us only one shot before we'd have to get another one. I figure we should wait to use it until tomorrow in case someone's already on his way here."

"What if that man comes back while we're gone?" Julianne asked.

"I realize it's not a very comforting thought, but whatever we do is a risk," David answered. "Let's go down to Tuesday's and buy what we need."

She was wary of visiting the general store, but she reluctantly agreed. What else could they do?

Petey greeted Julianne and David when they entered the general store. The cat meowed before rubbing against David's legs.

"Morning," David said, picking up the cat. "Do you have any batteries around here?"

Petey butted his head against David's chest in reply.

"Next to the candy," Ruby said between puffs of her cigarette. "What kind do you need?"

"Some for the—"

"Doesn't matter," Ruby said, cutting him off. "If we've got them, that's where they'll be."

David laughed as he carried the cat to the other side of the store.

Julianne watched Ruby for a moment. Perhaps she could glean some useful information from the store owner. "It's a pretty morning, isn't it?"

Ruby nodded, coughing out more smoke. "Yeah, I love the fresh air here."

Julianne chuckled to conceal a cough. "I assumed everything through here was privately owned, but we met that park ranger in here yesterday. Is this government land?"

"No," Ruby said. "We're on the edge of the park, but all of this is private."

"If this isn't part of the ranger's territory, why does he come out this way?" Julianne asked.

Ruby crushed out the stub of her cigarette. "He drops in now and again, probably to and from the park. Never buys much. He hasn't been around long. Not nearly as long as me." She laughed throatily. "But he's a ranger, so I suppose he's all right. He's never been any trouble. And Petey likes him, so I don't worry."

Julianne thought it wouldn't hurt to find out if anybody else had showed up here recently. She was careful to keep her expression neutral. "I guess you're right. You'd know more than anybody about things up here."

Ruby lit another cigarette. "It's going to be a hot one."

"Yeah, people like to get out of the city when it's hot," Julianne remarked. "You probably see a lot of newcomers stopping in, like me and Ray."

Ruby shrugged.

"What does Petey think of the heat?" Julianne asked, attempting to keep the conversation flowing.

"He's a big baby," Ruby answered. "He stays inside when it's too hot or cold."

Julianne smiled. "Have you always had cats? Or do you have dogs too?"

"I don't have time for big slobbery dogs," Ruby said, rolling her eyes. "Petey and I don't need them."

"If someone brought a dog out here lately, I suppose Petey would have noticed," Julianne said.

Ruby barked out a laugh. "Petey would hide in the storeroom and refuse to budge if a dog came within a mile."

Julianne sighed at the unhelpful response. "It must be pretty quiet around here, especially for summer."

"Oh, we have people in and out. Most of them I know. They're either locals or folks who come here every summer." Ruby stared at Julianne. "I don't tell their business, and they don't tell mine."

The subject was obviously closed. Julianne was disappointed that she hadn't learned anything, but hopefully that meant Ruby would be just as tight-lipped about their presence. "That seems fair."

David returned with the batteries. He was still carrying Petey. As soon as he set the cat on the counter, Petey jumped to the floor and vanished into the back room.

"Did you get pancake mix?" David asked eagerly.

"We've been talking." Ruby blew out another cloud of cigarette smoke and grinned at Julianne. "Go on. The food is next to the candy." She rasped out a laugh. "Most everything is."

"Thanks." Julianne walked to the other side of the store and found packaged chocolate cupcakes and a pancake mix that needed only the addition of water. She took a quart of milk and some butter out of the ancient refrigerator case, and then she remembered to get syrup.

By the time she rejoined them at the counter, David had collected two packs of playing cards, a travel checkers set with magnetic pieces, and a huge bag of beef jerky.

"Do you think that'll last you a day or two?" Julianne teased, pointing at the bag of jerky.

"I'll have to take it slow," he joked. "Did you get what we need?"

"I think so." She put everything down on the counter, then snagged an Agatha Christie novel from the rack near the counter and added it to the pile. "Can you think of anything else?"

David grinned at the jerky. "It seems about right to me."

"I'll sell you as much as you want," Ruby said as she finished ringing up their purchases. "As long as you can pay for it."

He handed her cash. "Keep the change. Buy something for Petey."

Ruby seemed thoughtful as she put their items into brown paper bags. "He did have an eye on some of that tuna we just got in."

"Tell him it's our treat," David said, taking the bags from her. "Thanks. We'll see you."

Julianne smiled at Ruby, glad to have had a moment of normalcy in the midst of all the craziness of the past week. With a start, she realized it hadn't even been an entire week. It seemed like forever now, as if the five months since David's supposed death had been brief and vague, and this was the lasting reality.

Julianne followed David out the door, but she stopped on the weathered front porch. She examined a nearly rusted-out metal sign advertising cola with a large thermometer attached to it.

He loaded the bags into the back seat, then called to her, "Ready?"

"It's already eighty-two," she said, motioning to the thermometer. "It's going to be warm in the cabin."

"Yeah, maybe I'd better get more ice." David hurried inside and reemerged with a five-pound bag of ice. "Ready now?"

"Yes." She walked with him to the car and got into the passenger seat.

They went back to the cabin. After David put away what they had bought, he started the generator to power the stove, then turned on the box fan.

Julianne mixed up the pancake batter and began cooking. Whoever had built the cabin a long time ago had made a wise choice in placing it under some lush oak trees. With the shade, the fan, and the breeze that blew through the building into the open front door and out the back, the cabin was relatively pleasant.

Soon they were seated at the small table with two generous plates of pancakes and cold glasses of milk to go with them.

They took their time eating, knowing it was going to be a long day with nothing to do.

Not for the first time, Julianne noticed him hiding a yawn. "How much sleep did you get last night?"

"I told you," David said. "I'm used to it."

She pursed her lips. "That means you didn't sleep at all, right?"

"Maybe," he admitted. "I don't know what we're up against. We may be fine for a long time. Or somebody might be on his way here any minute. I couldn't let someone walk in on us in the middle of the night."

"Are you planning to stay up again tonight?" Julianne asked, frowning.

"Possibly," he said.

She raised an eyebrow. "Wouldn't it make more sense if you got a few hours of sleep so you can stand guard tonight and not pass out?"

"You're right," David said. "I'll get some sleep, but you have to keep your eyes open and wake me up if you even suspect something is wrong."

"I will. I promise." Julianne stood and cleared the table. "After I clean up, I'll read my new book. Should we leave the generator on?"

"What do you think?" he asked. "Would you be comfortable without the fan?"

"I think so," she said after a moment's consideration. "Maybe we should save it for later when it gets hotter."

"Good idea." David went out to the back porch, and the hum of the generator and the fan died together.

When he returned, Julianne put her hands on her hips and stared at him until he went to the couch and stretched out.

David sat up and pulled the gun from his waistband. He set the gun on the floor within reach, stretched out again, and almost immediately went to sleep.

Satisfied that he was finally getting some much-needed rest, Julianne returned to the kitchen and washed up. Then in the shaded quiet of the cabin and under the filtered light from the front window, she held her book and kept watch.

She prayed that the rest of the day would be as peaceful as it was right now.

It was getting close to dark when David stirred. Julianne watched him as his regular deep breathing became shallower and less even. Suddenly, he sat bolt upright on the couch.

She froze, not wanting to startle him out of whatever he'd been dreaming, and waited for him to realize where he was and who she was.

A few moments later, David seemed to recognize her, and the tense breath seeped out of him. "I'm sorry, Julie."

Julianne's heart melted at the way he shortened her name like he used to. "Bad dream?" She went over and sat down on the sofa next to him, wrapping her arm around his. "I can't believe you slept through the thunderstorm."

"Is everything okay?"

"Yes, it's fine. The storm passed about an hour ago, and the temperature dropped. I haven't seen anyone outside."

"Good. It's time I got up." He stretched and rubbed his eyes. Then he went to the pump for cold water to splash on his face.

After that, he seemed completely awake. "Should we have some coffee and figure out what to do next?"

"That would be good," she said.

He fired up the generator, and she brewed the coffee. While they drank it, they both snacked on jerky and cupcakes at the table.

It was time to say what she'd been thinking. "Nobody's coming to help us, are they?"

David put an arm around her and pulled her close. "I'm going to use the phone. We'll figure out something. Just stay with me, all right? Trust me."

Her throat was clogged with tears, and she couldn't speak. Julianne wanted to trust him. She needed to trust him. But maybe he was in over his head. Maybe they had no way out of this nightmare.

He released her and got the burner phone. Two seconds later, he snapped it shut. "I should have known there'd be no signal up here. We'll have to get closer to a town. Somewhere with a cell tower. Come on."

Julianne slipped into her raincoat, and David slid the gun into his waistband and covered it with his jacket. They went out the back door.

As Julianne walked the short distance across the porch, one of the boards gave way under her foot. Pain shot through her ankle, and she stumbled forward, her arms flailing. She grabbed the rough post that supported the railing with her left hand. Splinters tore into her palm, and she cried out as a sharp pain pierced her hand.

David rushed to her side and tried to pull her upright, but she couldn't get her hand away from the post.

"Wait," Julianne gasped, tears springing to her eyes. "I'm stuck on something."

"Hold on. It'll be all right." He leaned over, regarded her hand, and winced. "Looks like you ran into a nail."

She glanced down and saw a stream of blood running down her arm and dripping off her elbow.

"I'm afraid this is going to hurt," David said, his eyes fixed on hers. "You need to hold still. Ready?"

Julianne nodded and bit her lower lip.

In one swift motion, he lifted her hand off the nail.

Tears streamed down her face from the agony, but she managed not to scream.

"I'm so sorry," David said as he helped her sit down on the generator box. "You stay right there for a minute." He darted into the cabin.

Reeling with pain, Julianne struggled to remain upright.

David returned with a large towel, and he used it to stanch the blood and tightly wrap her hand. He ushered her inside and settled her on a chair in the kitchen. Then he pumped fresh water into a serving bowl and brought it to the table. "Put your hand in here so we can see what we're dealing with."

She slowly placed her hand in the bowl. The cold water made her battered palm throb, and soon it was tinted a deep red.

"You got scraped up pretty good," David said as he carefully lifted her hand. "I wouldn't expect it to be anything serious. But this puncture wound might be a problem."

"I haven't had a tetanus shot," Julianne said.

"In that case, we need to take you to a doctor. A real one." He got the soap and the bag of medical supplies out of the bathroom and brought them to the table. "We don't have much to work with here, but we'll get you fixed up enough to take you into town."

"But we can't go to a doctor or a hospital," she argued. "It's too dangerous."

"We can't mess around with this," David said. "As far as I can tell, nobody knows where we are. There's no reason going to a clinic out here should attract attention. And if we don't, you're going to have serious problems. Now let's clean it up."

Julianne knew he was right. There was nothing else they could do.

He gently washed her hand in soap and water. With a sympathetic apology, he poured alcohol over it.

She screwed her eyes shut, unable to stop the tears from spilling out of them, especially when he poured alcohol directly into the puncture wound.

"I'm sorry," David said, wrapping her hand with the roll of bandages from the medical bag. He retrieved a fresh towel from the bathroom. "You can use that to pad your hand while we're driving. Are you okay?"

"Yes," Julianne lied. She managed a smile. "If we're going to go, we'd better get moving. Maybe we should stop and ask Ruby where the nearest clinic is."

"Good idea. We'll do that. I should be able to make my call once we're closer to town anyway." He pumped cold water over the bloodied towel, wrung it out, and left it to dry draped over the sink. Then he helped her to her feet.

Almost immediately, her left ankle throbbed, and she collapsed back into the chair.

David dropped to one knee and pushed up the leg of her jeans.

Julianne glanced down. Her ankle was scraped and already beginning to swell. "With the way my hand was hurting, I didn't realize my ankle was injured too. I don't think it's sprained, but it is twisted."

He swiftly cleaned and bandaged her ankle, then guided her to the car. Once he was behind the wheel, he turned the key.

Instead of the roar of the engine, there was a clicking sound.

"No," David said, pounding the steering wheel with both hands. "This can't be happening."

She groaned. "It's the battery, isn't it?"

"I'm sure it is. Maybe it's just a loose connection." He popped the hood and jumped out of the car. After a few minutes, he slid behind the wheel and tried the key again. Still, there was only clicking.

He shook his head. "It's not going anywhere. I'm sorry. We'll go down to Ruby's and see if she carries this kind of battery or a charger. If not, maybe she can give us a lift. We need to get you to the doctor."

Leaden fear dropped into the pit of her stomach. "I can't go with you."

"You can't stay here alone," David protested.

"Be reasonable," Julianne said. "I can't walk to the store with an injured ankle, and you can go a lot faster without me. It's not that far to Ruby's, and I'm sure she'll help you." She squeezed his arm with her good hand. "Please go. You need to hurry."

"Let me get you inside first." David grabbed the flashlight out of the glove box and ushered her into the cabin. After he helped her to the couch, he handed her the flashlight and the gun.

"No, you take the gun," she said as she accepted the flashlight. "Don't worry. I'll stay inside and be quiet and still. No one will even know I'm here."

"Are you positive?" he asked.

"Yes," Julianne said. "I don't know how to use it anyway, remember? Now please go." *Before I change my mind.*

"I'll be back as soon as I can." David picked up the lantern and exited through the rear door.

Julianne heard him open and close the trunk, and then she caught a glimpse of him as he ran past the side window and down the dim path.

In the darkness, she shivered and pulled her raincoat tighter. She kept the flashlight off, though she held it in case she needed it. She didn't know how long she sat there, waiting for him to return.

Please, God, keep David safe, Julianne prayed. *Bring him back to me soon.* Her hand and ankle throbbed. *Help me get to a doctor. Help me to remain strong and—*

Her heart leaped when she heard a car approach and saw a faint glow of headlights through the front curtains. A few moments later, she heard footsteps on the porch and the scrape of a key in the lock.

Julianne struggled to her feet, ready to switch on the flashlight and hurry into David's arms, but then she stopped herself. Obviously, he hadn't taken the car. What if Ruby hadn't brought him back? What if it was the park ranger? Or one of Fulton's men?

Silently, she dropped to the floor and crawled to the front wall. When Julianne peeked through the crack at the side of the curtain, she could see nothing but a hand and a sleeve and a belt through the loops of dark slacks. Blood pounded in her head when she remembered that David had been wearing jeans.

With her hand and ankle throbbing, Julianne hobbled to the back door, holding the heavy flashlight like a weapon, useless as it might prove to be.

Before she could escape the cabin, the front door burst open.

She whirled around to see a man standing in the doorway.

18

With her heart racing, Julianne froze and squinted into the light from the lantern the intruder held up.

The man lowered the lantern. "Are you okay?"

She let out a huge sigh of relief at the sight of Larry. "You scared me to death. What are you doing here?"

"I came to see if you were here," Larry said. "Mother and I were worried about you when you didn't come home, and then we found out that your boss hadn't heard from you."

"My boss?" Julianne echoed. Her heart began to race again. "Did you talk to him? I didn't know you knew him."

"I was out getting the mail when he stopped by your house," he explained. "You didn't answer the door, so he came over to talk to me."

"Did you tell him about this cabin?" she asked.

"No. I figured if you were skipping work, I should keep your little secret." Larry smiled, then motioned to her bandaged hand. "Did you hurt yourself?"

Julianne limped over to a chair and sat down. "One of the boards on the back porch broke, and I hurt my hand on the railing when I caught myself."

"You should get medical attention," he said.

"I was heading to the doctor, but my car won't start. I think the battery's dead."

"And your husband couldn't start it?" Larry asked. His mild eyes seemed strange in the yellow light that glinted off his thick glasses.

Shocked, Julianne stared at him, her mind whirling. All the pieces suddenly clicked into place. Larry was part of Fulton's operation. If Fulton's men had orchestrated her new job and house, then why wouldn't they plant Larry next door to watch her? It only made sense. Was Rhoda in on it too? Or was she clueless about what was going on?

"Your husband, David Montgomery," Larry said, his gentle and almost befuddled demeanor gone, replaced with one of cold determination. "I'm sure you remember him."

"David's dead," she said, trying to sound calm. "He was killed five months ago in a car accident—"

"Don't lie to me," he interrupted, his voice steely. "I know he's here with you."

"Did you stop by last night too?" Julianne asked, although she already knew the answer.

"Yeah, that was me, but I was interrupted by a phone call that I couldn't ignore." Larry smirked. "But this is even better. You're all alone, and David's out of the way."

She lifted her chin. "I don't know who you really are or what you want or what David's involved in. He showed up at my house in the middle of the night and made me get him out of Springfield. Now he's run out on me again, exactly like he did before."

"Sounds like your husband makes a habit of leaving you holding the bag," he remarked.

"He didn't care that I was hurt," Julianne continued. "All he cared about was getting away. I realized that somebody was after him, but he wouldn't tell me who or why. When the car wouldn't start, he took off. I thought he'd come back, but he hasn't."

Larry narrowed his eyes. "I want the rug."

Julianne attempted to keep her expression neutral. She didn't want to give away the fact that she knew which rug he was referring to. "What do you mean?"

"At your husband's supposed funeral, Macklin gave you a box of things from David's office," he said. "The rug was in there. I want it."

"I don't know what you're talking about," she insisted. "I lost everything in a fire in my house in Chicago. If I had the rug, it must have burned up then."

"You don't have much time," Larry warned. "We searched that house before it burned. The rug wasn't there. We searched your house in Springfield many times while you were at work. It wasn't there either. We thought that Macklin must have gotten it from you at some point, but we've discovered that he didn't have it. So, we're back to you. No matter where it's been before, you must have it with you now. I want it."

"I don't have it," Julianne said.

"I won't have a reason to keep you alive if you don't tell me where it is."

"Even if I tell you, you'll kill me anyway."

"If you tell me, I'll consider it a great favor," Larry said. "I'll take it, and Mother and I will simply disappear." He grinned. "People disappear all the time."

Julianne knew that Larry was lying. He'd kill her and bury her somewhere in the woods, and her body would never be found. "Why do you want it?" she asked, trying to stall for time.

"It's the key to Fulton's whole operation," he sneered. "There are several, but the FBI just needs one."

"What do you mean the rug is the key?" she asked. "That doesn't make any sense."

"I don't know," Larry said. "It's not my job. I was told to find it and bring it back to Paul Fulton before the feds get their hands on it and shut us down. Now tell me where it is. I don't want things to get ugly."

"It doesn't mean anything to me, and I don't care about this Fulton person or his business." Julianne lifted her unwounded hand appealingly. "Just don't kill me, all right? You can have the rug."

"Sure, you play nice with me, and nobody gets hurt."

She stood up, pretending her ankle hurt more than it did, and hobbled toward the back door. "I have no idea what David's been up to, and I don't care. If losing that stupid rug gets him in trouble, it's fine with me."

Larry snorted. "Works for me too. Where is it?"

"In the trunk," she answered, leading him outside. "To be honest, I didn't think anything about it. I assumed it was something Mr. Macklin was using to keep the things from David's office from getting broken. Neither of them told me anything."

"Yeah, isn't that the way it always is." He motioned toward the trunk. "Go ahead and open it."

"I don't have the keys," Julianne said. "David must have taken them with him. But I don't think it's locked. You can pop the trunk from inside. There's a handle by the driver's seat."

Without taking his eyes from her, Larry opened the driver's side door, leaned down, and pulled the handle. The trunk opened. He shut the door and steered her to the rear of the car. "Show me."

She pushed the trunk lid all the way up, not knowing what to do. Once Larry had what he was after, he wouldn't need her anymore. He would definitely kill her. There was no reason he wouldn't.

Larry held the lantern up while he rifled through the emergency supplies in the trunk. "Where is it?"

Julianne gasped. The rug was gone.

"What is this?" Larry demanded. "Where's the rug?"

"It was in the trunk," Julianne answered. "That's the last place I saw it."

"What are you trying to pull?" he snarled.

Julianne became frantic. She couldn't stall him anymore. He didn't care whether she knew anything about what David had been up to or not. He didn't care if she was in need of medical help. He just wanted the rug, and it was gone.

"Maybe it got pushed under something," she said, scanning the contents of the trunk. "Why don't you hold that light closer so I can see better?"

Larry leaned closer, moving the lantern deeper into the recesses of the trunk.

"David and I had some supplies in here," Julianne said, leaning closer too. "He might have shifted things around."

He laughed humorlessly as he shoved some things out of the way. "Ava said you were smart, and she insisted that we had to be careful around you. I can't wait to tell her how oblivious you've been."

"Who's Ava?" she asked.

"Mother," Larry said, his voice sickeningly sweet. "Dear Rhoda Spielmann."

"You mean she's not your mother?" she asked.

Larry snorted. "Hardly. She's been connected to Fulton since she was born. Her father was one of his father's lieutenants. She started working for Fulton as soon as she was old enough to carry a message, smuggle a package, and run a con."

So her other next-door neighbor was part of Fulton's operation too. Julianne thought of the older woman who had feigned concern for her and was always ready to lend a helping hand. "I'm assuming she's not wheelchair-bound."

"Not at all. The wheelchair made her seem harmless so you'd trust her. And her motherly act was another way to get close to you." He laughed. "Those so-called homemade dishes she was always giving you came from a catering place downtown. Ava can't even boil an egg."

"What about Buttons?" she asked. "Did someone poison her?"

"No, I was the one outside your house that night, trying to see if your husband was in there. What better way to cover that it was me than to claim the intruder had poisoned our dog to keep her quiet?"

"So, all of it was a setup." Julianne tried to sound bewildered and frightened as she slipped her good hand down into the trunk and wrapped her fingers around the tire iron. When Larry turned, she raised the tire iron. Before she could think about what she was doing, she struck him on the back of the head.

Larry grunted and fell to the ground.

Julianne had to get away before Larry regained consciousness. She took off around the side of the house and limped as fast as she could on her swollen ankle, reminding herself it wasn't broken or sprained.

Ruby's was the only place she could think of, so she headed in that direction. David had gone there, and she hoped he was on his way back. Larry hadn't seemed to know where he was, but someone else might have traveled here with Larry. Someone who'd already found David. Someone who'd captured him and maybe even killed him.

Julianne pushed the terrible scenarios away and focused on

escaping. Each step she took sent shooting pain through her ankle and up her leg, and every erratic beat of her heart throbbed through her punctured hand. Despite the excruciating pain, she forced herself to keep going. She had to. There wouldn't be any passersby to flag down for help. Julianne had to make it to Tuesday's on her own. She prayed that Ruby wasn't in on the conspiracy too.

She couldn't tell how far down the road she was. Halfway? A third? When Julianne realized she was moving more and more slowly with every jarring step, she finally veered off the road so she could lean against a tree. As she rested, she heard a car approaching from behind her. It wasn't coming from Tuesday's. It was coming from the cabin. Her breath hitched. It was Larry.

Julianne glanced over her shoulder. She couldn't see him yet, but she had to hide quickly. She had no choice but to duck into the trees. He couldn't follow her there, at least not in his car, and the trees were thick, especially with all the summer growth. She forced herself not to think of all the insects and spiders and wild animals in the burgeoning grass and brush. The overgrowth was her ally now, and so were the leafy, wind-tossed trees.

She took cover behind a tree right before Larry's brown four-door sedan came into view. She was sure he hadn't seen her.

But then the car slowed to a stop.

Heart racing, Julianne pressed her back against the tree trunk and waited. She didn't dare move, didn't dare breathe.

Finally, Larry pulled slowly forward.

Relief flooded her.

But it was quickly replaced by dread when the car swung around, its headlights sweeping through the trees.

"Julianne, I know you're out here," Larry called when he exited the car. "You're hurt, and you can't get away from me. When you move, I'll hear you in the brush, and there's nothing out that way but the edge of a ravine. If you come out and give me the rug, I won't hurt you."

Of course, Julianne wasn't fooled. She remained motionless. The wind was causing movement all around her, and she realized Larry wasn't quite sure where she was. Still, what was she going to do? She couldn't just stand there. He'd find her eventually. Julianne felt around with one foot until she came in contact with a large rock. She picked it up with her right hand and pressed herself against the tree again, waiting for her chance.

"There's nowhere for you to go now," Larry said. "You might as well come out."

Julianne held her breath, then threw the rock as hard as she could in the opposite direction, hoping to send him away from where she was hiding.

A moment later, she heard Larry jog toward the rock, so she silently went the other way, stepping as delicately as she could, trying to avoid the brush or anything that would rustle too much. The wind picked up a little, making the whole forest sway, and she moved away from Larry and his headlights, still heading toward Ruby's and help. If not help, at least witnesses. She hadn't seen anyone but the ranger in the store when she and David had been there, but Ruby must get other customers. *Please, God, let someone be there.*

"I found your trail," Larry said from behind her.

He sounded farther behind her than before, but she was sure that he was gaining on her.

Julianne could feel herself faltering. Her leg ached even more, and she began to stumble. What else could she do but keep moving? If she stopped, she'd be dead. Where could she go where he wouldn't find her?

Larry had mentioned a ravine alongside the road. A dead end for sure. He wouldn't expect her to go that way. Wouldn't he assume that she would continue toward Tuesday's and help? She swerved to her left, attempting to step quietly and move stealthily. The summer plants were healthy and supple, and it was dark. She prayed that he wouldn't be able to tell where she'd gone.

As Julianne kept going, she heard Larry calling to her. Was he farther away now? Down the path past her? She didn't slow down, at least not intentionally, but her steps became increasingly unsteady. Her hand throbbed fiercely. She had to stop somewhere. But where?

Ahead of her, she spotted a swath of darkness, a deep nothingness that opened the ground a few feet away. The ravine. She was trapped.

But she hadn't heard anything from Larry in a while, so maybe he'd moved on.

Before Julianne could breathe a sigh of relief, she spotted the bobbing light of his lantern in the woods behind her, and she knew he was still on her trail. He hadn't been fooled. Not for long anyway.

Julianne needed to move faster. She tried to run, but her ankle gave way, sending her sprawling. When she landed on the ground, a spike of pain shot through her hand, and she felt her bandage turn warm and wet. What now? She gazed up to the dark heavens. *Oh, God, please help me.*

The tree above her was a broad-spreading oak. If she could pull herself up to the first branch, she could perch on it and hide. Maybe Larry wouldn't think she'd climb a tree, and she was certain he wouldn't be able to see her there at night.

She struggled to her feet and approached the base of the tree. Her jump was torture to her ankle. Grasping the branch was agony to her scraped hands. Julianne ignored the pain and focused on her mission of climbing the tree and disappearing in the branches. Maybe Larry would give up and go away. She wished now that she had thought to bring the tire iron with her. She wished she'd let David leave the gun with her. Sure, she couldn't use it, but Larry wouldn't know that. Maybe she could have bluffed with it.

"Julianne!" Larry yelled. He sounded closer, and the light from the lantern bounced through the trees.

She gingerly climbed two more branches and stopped. He was in the clearing below her, surrounded by lantern light, repeatedly calling her name.

"I'll find you," Larry said. "Even if it takes all night, I'll find you." He studied the ground for a moment, then laughed.

The sound made her blood run cold. What had he found?

"I can see where you've been," he said. "Here's where you fell. It's too bad that you're bleeding again. Puncture wounds like that are very dangerous if they're not treated. Tetanus is a nasty disease to catch."

Larry continued studying the ground as he stalked over to the tree where she was hiding. He raised the lantern and looked up at her. "You should come down. It's no use being stubborn now that I've found you. Tell me where the rug is, and I'll make sure you get the medical treatment you need. I think that's a fair deal."

Even though he stared directly at her, Julianne didn't move or say a word.

Larry pulled a gun from the shoulder holster under his jacket and pointed it at her. "I can shoot you as easily up there as on the ground. Now tell me where the rug is."

"I swear it was in the trunk," Julianne answered. "I don't know anything else about it except what you told me. I thought it was just something Macklin put in that box of David's things to keep them from getting broken. Killing me won't help anything."

"All right, I believe you," he said. There was a touch of regret in his expression as he took careful aim at her. "But that doesn't mean I can let you walk away and tell the police about all this."

She put out one hand. "Please don't shoot!"

"Is this what you're searching for?" David stepped into the clearing across from Larry, his back to the ravine. He clutched the rolled-up rug to his chest.

"So, you had it all along," Larry said.

"Not all along," David said. "All the time you and Fulton's guys were trying to flush me out, Julianne had it. All you had to do was break into her car one day when she was at work, and she probably would have never noticed it was gone."

"Fulton thought Macklin had passed it to you," Larry said. "By the time we realized he'd given it to her, you were already back and on the run. None of that matters, though. Hand it over, and we'll call it quits."

"I have a better idea," David said. "If you don't let us go, I'll throw the rug into the ravine, and you'll never get it back."

"That's all right," Larry responded. "I don't need it. I only have to make sure that nobody else can ever get it."

"Guess again," David said. "If I toss it down there, a dozen FBI agents will soon be swarming the area. They'll find the rug before you can tell your boss where it is. And it will be your fault when his whole operation is ripped wide open."

"Give it to me," Larry spat.

David stepped backward, closer to the ravine. "Let my wife go."

"Don't get any closer to the edge," Larry warned.

David set his jaw.

Julianne knew that look. He wasn't going to budge. "David, please give it to him."

"Stay where you are," David told her, then faced Larry. "What's it going to be? Let her go, and I'll give you the rug."

"You know I can't let her go," Larry said.

"So I'll have to toss the rug," David said as he took another step back.

"Stay away from the edge," Larry ordered. He pointed the gun at David and pulled the trigger.

The horrific sound of a gunshot split the air, and David collapsed to the ground.

"N o!" Julianne clung to the tree, the rough bark scraping her cheek as she sobbed against it. She felt dizzy. She couldn't believe that Larry had shot David in cold blood.

Larry turned to her and raised the gun. "There's no reason to keep you alive now. I have what I want. But don't worry. You and your husband will be together again."

She clung more tightly to the tree, her gaze fixed on David. Her vision was blurred, and all she could make out was his dark, huddled form in the tall grass.

Larry aimed the gun at her.

Julianne closed her eyes and braced herself. She flinched at the shot, then opened her eyes. It was Larry who fell. With a gasp, she glanced toward the ravine and saw David jumping to his feet. He was alive. Her heart raced at the thought of how close they had both come to being killed.

After striding over to Larry, David dropped to one knee, took the gun from Larry's outstretched hand, and stuck it into the back of his belt. He pressed his fingers against the side of Larry's neck. "He's dead."

She scrambled down the tree as quickly as her battered ankle and scraped hands would let her, then lowered herself from the bottom branch.

David caught her and wrapped her in his arms, holding her close. "Are you okay?"

"Are *you* okay?" Julianne asked, laughing and crying at the same time.

He nodded.

Julianne touched his face and searched his eyes. She stepped back, examining him in the low light of the lantern Larry had dropped. "How badly are you hurt?"

"Only a little bruised," David said. He showed her the rug with two bullet holes in it.

"You had your gun hidden in there," Julianne said. "But it couldn't have protected you from getting shot."

"I was holding it in front of my bulletproof vest," he said.

"I was too relieved to even notice," she admitted. "I can't believe you're alive again."

David grinned. "Third time's a charm, don't you think?"

"I hope so," Julianne said. She hugged him tightly. "Thank you for saving my life."

"I wasn't about to let Larry shoot you over a stupid rug."

She stepped back and regarded it. "This isn't even the same rug."

"I removed the real one from the trunk and took it with me to Ruby's," he said. "In case something happened, I thought you'd be safer without it, but I was wrong about that."

"I don't understand," Julianne said. "Where did you get another rug and a bulletproof vest?"

"At Tuesday's," David answered, sounding a bit smug. "Don't you know they carry everything?"

"No way."

"I'll tell you everything later," he promised. "We need to get you to a doctor."

"How will we get there?" she asked. "The battery's dead."

"At this point, I don't think Larry will mind if we use his car."

Julianne shuddered as she glanced at Larry sprawled out in the grass, his hand still outstretched and his glasses twisted across his face.

"Let's go," David urged.

Leaning on her husband, she started to hobble to the road, but David swung her into his arms and carried her through the brush.

Julianne let herself relax and rested her head on his shoulder. She pressed her face against his neck, breathing in the well-remembered scent of him, feeling the steady beat of his heart and the warmth of his skin. Oh, how she'd missed him.

When they made it to the road, Larry's sedan was parked in the same place, its engine idling and headlights shining into the trees.

David settled her into the passenger seat.

Julianne closed her eyes. Being in Larry's car made her feel a little sick, but maybe she was feeling a little sick anyway. At least it was a relief to sit down.

"Are you all right?" he asked as he got into the driver's seat.

"I'm glad this is over," she said, buckling her seat belt. "It is over, isn't it?"

Before he could answer, a jeep pulled up beside them.

Julianne recognized the park ranger they'd seen at Tuesday's. What in the world was he doing here?

David left the car, walked over to the ranger, and leaned into his open passenger window.

After a few minutes, the ranger drove into the grass at the edge of the road and parked. With his headlights pointed toward the dark woods, he marched into the trees.

David returned to the car and shut the door.

"What did the ranger say?" Julianne asked. "Why was he even here?"

"His name is Brad Collins," he replied. "He'll see to the body and make sure nobody else is around here searching for us. He said the local clinic is waiting for us. They won't ask for any ID. All we have to do is tell them we're Ray and Kit Sherman."

"So the ranger is the contact you've been waiting for?" Julianne asked.

"No, but our contact sent him."

"What do you mean?"

"We're safe for now, and all the explanations can wait," David said. "Get some rest while we drive to the clinic."

She nodded and sank into the cushioned seat, suddenly more exhausted than she'd ever been in her life.

As David had promised, the clinic was waiting for them with no questions asked. Kit Sherman and her husband, Ray, were escorted into an examination room immediately.

Julianne's ankle was x-rayed, diagnosed as a slight sprain, and tightly wrapped. Her hand was also x-rayed, and the wound was carefully cleaned and sewn up. The doctor gave her a tetanus shot along with pain medication, instructions on how to care for her injuries, and orders to follow up with her own doctor. There was no charge.

"It's all taken care of," the nurse said with a smile. "And you have a visitor." She opened the exam room door and left.

Ruby strolled inside.

Julianne gaped at her, then sat up straighter in her chair.

"What? You think I'm chained to my cash register or something?" Ruby patted her shirt pocket as if searching for her cigarettes, then scowled. "Anyway, they say you'll be fine."

"Yes, thank goodness," Julianne said.

"You had a close call out there," Ruby commented.

Puzzled, Julianne turned to David. He was obviously attempting to hide a sly smile.

"Oh, the ranger told me everything when he came down to the store to wait for backup," Ruby said. "Somebody had to clean up the mess you two made."

Julianne faced David again. "What's going on?"

"Ruby's our contact," he announced.

"Really?" Julianne asked, stunned. She never would have guessed that the older woman was the agent Mack had sent to help them. Ruby had been at the lake all the time, acting like she couldn't have cared less. "How did you find out?"

"We got connected when I arrived at the general store and told her that you were hurt," David said.

"We had already visited your store twice," Julianne told Ruby. "So how did you realize that David was the person you were supposed to help?"

"When I talked to Macklin, he described the rug Becker put in the box along with the things from your husband's office," Ruby said. "I noticed that David was carrying that rug, so I mentioned Savannah. When he responded in the right way, I knew it was him."

"Just in time," Julianne said. "Then what happened?"

"Brad picked me up at Ruby's," David replied. "We saw Larry's car on the road, and we knew he must have been after you. Brad dropped me off so I could come up along the ravine and check out the situation. We wanted to take Larry alive, but he gave me no choice."

"Is that going to be a problem?" Julianne asked.

Ruby shook her head. "There's enough evidence on him and his so-called mother to connect them to Fulton's organization."

"I can't believe that I trusted my neighbors," Julianne said. They'd acted so concerned, but they had only been spying on her.

"They were good actors," David said.

Julianne felt light-headed. Suddenly, she remembered her boss. "What about Jim Webber?"

David touched his wife's shoulder. He hated to break the news to Julianne that her boss was responsible for destroying their home. "Ray Gist, otherwise known as Jim Webber, will be arrested for his involvement in Fulton's operation as well as for arson."

"Arson?" Julianne repeated, her voice cracking.

He nodded. "He's the one who burned down our house."

"But he was always so nice to me." Tears fell down Julianne's cheeks, and she wiped them away.

David took her hand and squeezed it. He wished he could do something to take away all the pain he had caused her. "You should get some rest. We can talk about it later."

"No, I have so many more questions," Julianne said. She released his hand and leaned forward. "Where's the real rug?"

"I left it with Ruby," David said.

Ruby nodded. "I passed it on to Brad."

"How did you know to take it to her?" Julianne asked David.

"I didn't," he admitted. "But I didn't want to leave it where it was when you were at the cabin alone."

"Why is the rug so important?" Julianne asked.

"Evidently there's a code woven into it," he said. "Once they break the code, the bureau will be able to figure out how Fulton's money-laundering operation works, including the names of their contacts and account numbers. Paul will soon be joining his father in prison."

"That's a relief," Julianne said.

"Mack must have discovered something about Becker and the rug after he talked to me," David said. "But he was killed before he could tell me."

"The bureau's investigating who was out to get Macklin," Ruby said. "We learned about the rug and what it was used for. All we can do is assume Becker wanted that rug out of his own hands and with someone who didn't have a clue what it meant."

"That was you," David told Julianne. "Becker was probably planning to tell someone he could trust where the rug was, but somebody killed him before he could do it. Now I'm not sure whether that was one of Fulton's guys or one of ours."

"What will happen to Porter?" Julianne asked.

"Porter's being picked up right now for the murder of Macklin," Ruby said, her eyes hard. "I hate a traitor."

"With my testimony, he'll definitely be put away," David assured Ruby. "Besides betraying the bureau, he'll have to answer to at least one murder charge. And you can go back to your quilting group."

"Ms. Truvay is the one who quilts." Ruby smiled. "I teach gun safety at the shooting range."

"Wait," Julianne said, sounding baffled. "You're not Ms. Truvay?"

"Agent Louise Metzger, retired," Ruby said by way of introduction. "The FBI makes us retire when they think we're too old. Every once in a while, they rehire us when they need somebody with experience and ability."

"And somebody inconspicuous," David put in.

"Where's the real Ruby?" Julianne asked.

"Getting pampered for a week at a resort spa under an alias," Louise said. "I promised her nothing would happen to Petey while she was gone. At least nothing but being spoiled rotten."

David chuckled.

"The bureau is grateful to you both," Louise said, then nodded at David. "I'm sure we could get you situated in a new position without much trouble."

"I don't know," he said.

"It would be a shame to lose a good agent like you," Louise said.

"It's time I reevaluate what I really want to do." David glanced at his wife. "Consider what's most important." He hoped Julianne would give him another chance. There was nothing he wanted more than to share the rest of his life with her.

"I'm not the one who makes the decisions, of course," Louise said, "but I'm sure the offer stands if you ever decide to return."

"We'll see," he said.

"Give it some thought," Louise said. "For now, I need to get back to the store and make sure Petey gets his roast chicken." She waved and walked out of the room.

After Louise left the exam room, Julianne remarked, "She must have been something when she was a full-time agent."

"She still is." David sat down in the chair beside her. "Thanks to her and Brad, we made it out of a real jam."

She breathed out a huge sigh of relief. "I can go home."

"You can never return to Springfield," he said soberly.

"It doesn't matter," Julianne said. "I don't have a home anymore. I don't even have a real job."

"When you're up to it, we'll have to be debriefed by the bureau," he said. "They'll need to know everything that happened and what we found out. I'll have to give them a detailed statement about what I saw at Mack's house."

"What happens after we testify?" she asked.

"We won't be able to be David and Julianne Montgomery anymore."

"Why not?"

"Mike Fulton is still running things from his prison cell," David explained. "Even with Paul in there with him, somebody else will be after us. We'll both have to go into witness protection and assume new identities."

"New identities?" Julianne echoed.

"You can't be Mrs. Montgomery anymore, but you don't have to be Mrs. Anyone." He studied her. "Not if you don't want to be."

She blinked. Was he letting her choose or letting her go? How could she lose him again, after just getting him back? Even though he'd broken her heart, he'd saved her life twice, and she knew she could trust him to keep protecting her. With a jolt, she realized that she didn't care what happened as long as they were together. "What are you going to do?"

"Like I told Ruby, I need to think about it," David said. "I shouldn't have kept you in the dark about my work or left you home alone so often. I don't want another job that puts me in that position. What about you?"

"I'm not sure what to do," she said after a moment.

"What would you do if you could do anything you wanted to?" He took her hand. "If you weren't afraid to fail?"

Julianne had already considered this question. "I'd live on an island and paint," she said, the light of possibility shining before her. "I'd open a charming bed-and-breakfast and watch the rest of the world go by."

"Do you need somebody to help run the place?" David asked, his expression hopeful. "Maybe somebody who could be head of security?"

Julianne laughed and threw her arms around his neck. "Absolutely. Do you happen to know anyone who might be interested?"

"What about me?" he asked.

"I'll have to think it over," she teased.

David smiled, then gazed deeply into her eyes. "I love you so much."

"I love you too," she whispered. "You've always been the only one for me."

"Even if I can't always tell you what's going to happen next?" he asked.

"Nobody can do that," Julianne said. "But it's all right, as long as we're honest with each other from now on and face everything together."

"I promise," David murmured.

Then he kissed her, sealing his vow, and the rest of the world faded away.

Up to this point, we've been doing all the writing. Now it's *your* turn!

Tell us what you think about this book, the characters, the bad guy, or anything else you'd like to share with us about this series. We can't wait to hear from *you*!

Log on to give us your feedback at:
https://www.surveymonkey.com/r/sweetintrigue

Annie's FICTION